CHASING A CHANCE

WESTERN HISTORICAL ROMANCE - A KIOWA WELLS STORY

ANGELA RAINES

CHINOOK MOUNTAIN PUBLISHING

CONTENTS

1. Chapter 1 — 1
2. Chapter 2 — 9
3. Chapter 3 — 15
4. Chapter 4 — 23
5. Chapter 5 — 31
6. Chapter 6 — 37
7. Chapter 7 — 47
8. Chapter 8 — 55
9. Chapter 9 — 61
10. Chapter 10 — 71
11. Chapter 11 — 79
12. Chapter 12 — 87
13. Chapter 13 — 95

14. Chapter 14   105

15. Chapter 15   111

16. Chapter 16   117

17. Chapter 17   129

18. Chapter 18   137

19. Chapter 19   147

20. Chapter 20   153

21. Chapter 21   161

22. Chapter 22   167

23. Chapter 23   173

24. Chapter 24   187

25. Chapter 25   191

26. Chapter 26   199

27. Chapter 27   209

28. Chapter 28   217

29. Chapter 29   223

30. Chapter 30   233

31. Chapter 31   245

32. Author's Notes   249

Afterword   251

CHAPTER I

"You remember Mary Winters, Win?" Chet asked, using the name he'd always used since he and Edwin Markham had been kids. "Well she ran off after her husband was killed," he continued, his voice echoing in his drink.

At the sound of Mary's name, Edwin stopped listening and fell into his memories. Oh, how he'd admired and loved her. He thought of her smile, her laughter as he fingered the locket he always carried in his pocket. He'd bought it for Mary as a gift, while he'd been away during the war. While on a short leave in St. Joseph, Missouri, he'd entered a small shop, The Bavarian Jewelry and Watch Repair Shop, to get his watch repaired. It was there he'd seen the locket. The proprietor, a German fellow, had the locket for sale that was just perfect for Mary. As Edwin talked about Mary, the man told Edwin it would be perfect. Edwin agreed and purchased it for her.

He'd never given it to her. Mary had married Howard Gilpin while he was gone. Some would have said he had a right to be angry, to hate her, but no words of love had been exchanged. He'd been too shy, too naïve about women to let her know. Still, he had the locket. He'd kept it. It hadn't felt right to send it to her after she'd married. Now it was a reminder of that innocence of childhood.

To ease the pain, he'd stayed away. He cared too much to be around, but in his heart, he wished her well when he'd heard. He still remembered her blue eyes and imagined how happy she must have been that day at the church. He knew Howard was a good man and had a good job at the bank. Edwin knew Mary would be taken care of.

He'd told no one he was planning to join up. He'd felt the need to help preserve the Union. He didn't want anyone to keep him from doing his duty, or cry because he left. Now after all these years, he heard her name again, although he'd never stopped thinking of her.

You listenin' to me, Win?" Chet demanded, glancing at Edwin from the corner of his eye.

"What?" Edwin shot a startled look at Chet, "I was woolgathering," he finished with an embarrassed grin.

"I was saying that no good bank owner, he blamed Howard for taking the bank's money. Claimed the others had killed Howard so's they wouldn't have to share. Turns out he's the one who killed Howard. Never were no others."

"What bank robbery? When did this happen? How did Mary take it?" Edwin interrupted Chet's ramblings, each question falling on top of the one before it.

"What?"

"What about Mary, when did this occur?" Edwin asked, struggling to keep his voice even. Thoughts of Mary, of what happened to her, clouded his thinking. She had to be okay. "Was she okay?"

"Mary's fine," Chet mumbled, burying his face in the glass.

Grabbing Chet by the collar, Edwin whirled him around, "Chet, dammit, why are you avoiding my question? Did..."

Chet averted his eyes, unwilling to look at Edwin. Edwin's heart dropped to his toes. His mother taught him before she'd died of consumption, that life didn't always treat people fairly. He understood that, but what might have happened to Mary...the thought tightened his muscles and his grip on Chet.

Chet put his hands up, trying to loosen the chokehold Edwin had him in. No matter how hard he tried, Chet couldn't get the leverage to loosen Edwin's hold. The few bystanders in the bar just kept out of the way. They knew and respected Edwin. If he was manhandling this man there must be a good reason.

"Edwin, Edwin," Chet croaked, the world getting darker and darker, as he felt himself falling.

"Don't you pass out on me," Edwin growled, pulling Chet up, leaning him against the bar. "What in God's name happened to Mary?"

"She left, about a month after it happened, "bout twenty years ago," Chet gasped out. "The townsfolk believed she'd taken off with the money."

"Did you try to help her? Did anyone believe her?" Edwin demanded, his grip growing tighter as fear for Mary overwhelmed his thoughts.

Chet's chin dropped, his body sinking as he lost consciousness.

"You....," Edwin snarled, loosening his hold on Chet's throat, slapping the man to bring him back. As Chet's eyes opened, Edwin snarled. "Why are you telling me this after all these years?"

Chet tried to jump back, hands raised in defeat. "I saw her recently. She didn't recognize me, but I know'd it was her."

"Where did you see her? It's been over twenty years. Are you sure it was her?" Each question fell faster and faster as Edwin struggled to not choke Chet, angry and scared at the same time. Mary, his Mary, in trouble. He needed to know more.

"Yes, I'd know that red hair and blue-eyed combination anywhere," Chet whispered, his vocal cords bruised from the choke-hold. "Why you so upset?"

"I can't believe that she was treated like that," Edwin growled, his hands tightening their hold on Chet's collar, loosening only as Chet started to fall forward.

"If you're so worried, why not go help her, just don't ask me for anything," Chet gasped, glaring at Edwin. He grabbed his drink and, draining the glass, hurried from the bar. When he'd seen his childhood friend Edwin, Chet was thrilled for more reasons than one. Now he couldn't get away fast enough. Chet was almost through the door when he was brought up short with a hand on his shoulder.

"Chet, where did you see her? Why would I need to help her?" Edwin knew he'd frightened Chet, but the mention of Mary brought back so many memories, memories he'd kept safe. Now, he couldn't let Chet go without finding out where Mary was. He had to admit, he'd never stopped loving her.

"Was she in trouble? You're avoiding answering my question," Edwin's voice rose in frustration as he watched Chet's eyes, daring him to tell the truth.

"She's living in a small town in the southeastern part of the state. She runs a general store," Chet quickly answered.

Edwin loosed a breath he hadn't realized he was holding. Mary was doing okay. The pride he felt at her resilience surprised even him. Then another question popped into his head, "Chet, which town?"

"Booming," Chet replied pulling loose from Edwin, he moved out the door. "Now my turn for a question. Wasn't you with the Iowa Light Infantry?"

"Yes, but are you sure of the town name?" Edwin asked, but Chet had already left, forgetting that last question as he focused on Mary. As he repeated the town name he remembered stories coming from that part of the state, the murders, the outlaws crossing from no man's land, taking what they wanted, and escaping before the law could catch them. If Mary was there, how safe was she?

Heading to his store, Edwin began making plans. The new lady he hired could manage the place for a while. He was going to Booming.

Edwin was so involved with his plans he failed to see or hear the rumble of the horses until a shout of anger hit his ears. He barely heard the "is he dead" as the red haze changed to nothing. The clip of the horse's hoof drove him down a long dark tunnel. He saw Mary again at the end of that tunnel, just as she'd looked when he'd last seen her.

CHAPTER 2

"When you're ready, fire away," Stu laughed.

Mary stood inside her store, horrified at the callous disregard the men who'd overrun the town had for anyone. Watching the one they called Stu force the gun into seven-year-old Bobby's hand and demand he shoot brought up a wave of anger she hadn't felt for years.

"What if I miss?" young Bobby asked, his hand shaking with the weight of the pistol and possibly fear.

"Well, just keep firing. You'll eventually hit something. You get six tries," Stu laughed, then jumped back when Bobby accidentally turned the gun toward him. "But not me!" he shouted, shoving the gun away and toward Tad, another child who'd been playing with Bobby.

Unable to let the scene continue, Mary could keep quiet no longer. It was bad enough the town was hiding behind their doors, justifiably fearful of these men. But to allow their children to be subjected to the games of these same men was outside enough. She marched out the door of her general store and grabbed the gun from Bobby's hand. She then pointed it at Stu's face, the anger giving her strength to hold the heavy gun, declaring, "Take your games and foolishness somewhere else and leave the children alone."

Perhaps it was the surprise that saved her, for Mary continued, smiling as she sweetly said, the gun still under Stu's nose, "Should I give it a try? Shall I keep shooting until I hit something?"

Stu stared at Mary, his hulking bear shape reminding her of how dangerous that animal was when waking from sleep. Still, she was not going to back down. She'd run once, a long time ago, and had declared to herself *never again*. Grimly she held the gun steady with both hands now, her finger on the trigger.

"Well, you caught me napping," Stu grinned, but made no move to take the gun, or any other aggressive move, "but there are more of us than you, ma'am."

Mary watched Stu, aware that her actions were fraught with dire consequences, but she was not going to back down. To do so would defeat her purpose. These men would continue threatening, but she would not allow them to abuse the children.

"Maybe so," Mary said, the barrel steady as she continued, "but I will manage to take some of you with me."

Without turning her eyes from the men in front of her, Mary told Bobby and Tad to head home. She watched the others as their eyes followed the boys. She could tell they were waiting for a sign from Stu, a sign that never came.

"You might have caught me napping, but..." Stu repeated, adding, "besides the boss might take a dim view of killing women, especially you."

"But it would have been okay for young Bobby to accidentally kill me?" Mary challenged.

Stu stared at Mary, his gray eyes oddly warming, suddenly he burst out laughing. After a moment the others followed suit.

"I'll be damned, she's got us there." He bowed to Mary, and turning, headed away.

Mary began to relax when Stu suddenly turned and drew his other pistol, thumbing back the hammer to fire. He stopped before pulling the trigger as he heard the click of the gun in Mary's hand.

"Just kidding," he said, replacing the gun in its well-worn holster. "I'll be back later for my gun." Motioning to the others, they all trooped off.

Mary stood rooted where she was watching the procession move to the next street where the saloons stood. Only after the last one entered The Kingdom, the fanciest one, did she move. Turning, the pistol began to waver as she began shaking uncontrollably. Placing the pistol in her apron pocket, Mary returned to her store. Once inside, she braced herself against the brick wall, its strength comforted and supported her, calmed her.

"What kind of fool are you?" the banker's wife, Agnes, demanded as she shoved her head into the doorway, her hazel eyes condemning. Without waiting for an answer, she sniffed and stared at Mary. Getting no response, the woman sniffed and moved away.

Mary watched Agnes as she moved away, pity mixed with scorn for the woman. "You'll rue the day you..." Mary heard Agnes say as she moved to shut the door. Shaking her head, Mary observed Agnes parade down the street to her husband's bank.

Moving away from the wall, she walked farther into her store. The coolness, the vinegary smell of pickles, the pungent odor of the coffee doing much to bring the calm she sought. Perhaps she should try harder to get along with people like Agnes, but she found it hard to deal with people who were too frightened to stand up for themselves, let alone children.

"Would you have interfered if it had been Agnes or someone like her?" Mary asked the silent wall.

When the wall didn't answer, Mary smiled. "I would have been surprised if you had," she told the same wall. The bricks stood solid, not judging, just watching the foolishness of the people around, both inside and out. The wall would still be there long after they all ceased to be.

"What you must have seen," Mary continued, "but if I am honest with myself, I would've done the same thing no matter who it was, if they were unable to defend themselves. You have to take a stand, regardless of what you think the outcome might be."

The rest of the day passed uneventfully, which Mary was thankful for. She kept busy filling orders for her customers. No one mentioned the incident, but she could tell by the way they had looked at her the story was getting around. *Perhaps it will spur some of them to take action,* she thought but knew better.

After locking up, Mary moved toward her living quarters in the back of the store. She cast a final look outside before turning the corner. The street was empty, the sky starting to shift toward night. Fixing herself a small meal, Mary sat at the table thinking about Bobby and Tad. Her mind wandered back to her son, the son she gave up before she could get to know him. "I hope he never had to deal with men like this," she said as she cleaned the dishes and prepared for who knew what fresh hell would happen once the liquor took hold and night settled in.

Thinking back, she realized she would do it all again, go out into danger if the situation arose.

As she blew out the light, a series of shots rang through the night. She jumped as she heard the thud of one hitting the brick wall outside.

CHAPTER 3

Four days later, Edwin was finally on his way. It was three days later than he'd planned, but Doc Josie wouldn't let him leave until his dizziness had passed. Oh, he'd tried to fool her, but as most folks around Kiowa Wells learned, you didn't try to argue or put one over on the good doctor. Edwin didn't mind. He trusted Josephine and her husband Will, who was the law for Kiowa Wells and the surrounding area. They'd helped him get started when he moved into the area, after buying the mercantile and feed store.

Edwin found a pleasant place to stop in a stand of cottonwood near the Arkansas River. He'd just forded the river as the sun was painting the western sky with red, purple, and yellow. He wanted to keep going but knew if

he rushed in, he might walk into more problems than he could handle. Despite his desire to
reach Booming and Mary, he wanted to arrive
with an understanding of the area. He wanted to observe what was happening as best he
could. The more he knew, the better he would
help—could help—Mary. That was the story he
told himself as he made camp and began to
prepare his meal.

The truth was, he wasn't sure he was up for
what he might have to do. Sure, he'd been in
the war and survived. Now, he was an old man
who'd spent the years since the war, chasing
one dream after another. When he'd been shav-
ing before he'd set out the face looking back at
him in the mirror looked at least twenty years
older than his actual age. If things got physi-
cal with whoever was taking over the town, he
didn't know if he had what it took to prevail.
What if he had to kill someone? He'd sworn
after the war that he was done with violence,
yet he'd so easily attacked Chet. What was he
doing? Could he do anyone any good?

Edwin thought about the stories coming from
that lower southeast section of the state. The
stories of gangs from the Nation, of conflict
about where the county seat would be. Was any

of it true or just exaggerations of something small? The more he could find out, the better he felt he could handle what was happening. He just prayed it wasn't as bad as he'd heard

Edwin was lying back against his saddle, holding the locket, taking in the evening sounds. He enjoyed the soothing sound of the river, along with the other sounds he rarely heard in town. Into his reverie came the clip-clop of a horse. He pocketed the locket and sat up to see who it might be, but was not alarmed. Whoever was coming would have smelled his smoke even if they hadn't seen his fire. He'd usually been able to talk his way through any situation. The horse came closer, heading toward his camp. The only sign of worry Edwin showed was a bit of perspiration on his upper lip. He had his hunting rifle, but that was only to be used as a last resort. He hoped to never use it against a human.

"Hello the camp," came the call from the twilight outside the fire's glow.

"Come on in, if you've a mind," Edwin replied, tracking the sound of the horse as it neared the fire.

Into the light of the fire, came a man riding a beautiful chestnut. As the man and horse came into the light, Edwin thought the man looked fairly young, possibly in his early twenties. Edwin watched the man as his eyes took in the camp and surrounding area, only when he finished did he look directly at Edwin. Yet somehow Edwin knew the man was aware of his readiness to deal with any problems, despite his not having a weapon. It wasn't that he would win, but he was prepared. The thought gave Edwin some encouragement in himself, something he was going to need where he was headed if the stories proved to be true.

"You seem mighty careful," the man said, but a genuine smile took away any sting his words might have caused.

"Hear it can be downright unhealthy for some folks around here. I'd rather not be one of them."

The young man laughed, taking the measure of the man before him. He made a snap decision and confessed, "That's why I'm heading this way. Going to Booming. I took the US Deputy marshal job for this region. Thought I'd sort of do some moseying around, check things out, you know before I officially ride into town."

Edwin smiled to himself. It seemed this man was doing the same thing as himself. He wondered what had made the young man so wise. "You're being mighty cautious. I'd say that's pretty smart, but what if I was one sent to spy or await you?"

"No, you wouldn't be one of them, you got an honest look about you," the young man answered. "Besides, being cautious and assessing folk is the best way I know to stay alive. How's about some coffee?"

"Help yourself," Edwin answered. He found he liked the young man, watching him as he reached for the pot on the stone near the fire. There was something about him that was solid, and at the same time familiar.

The two sat in comfortable silence. Edwin leaned back again, relaxing against his saddle. The young man noticed and gave a slight smile, saluting Edwin with his cup.

Taking a last drink of his coffee, the young man stood, "Well, thanks for the coffee. I won't say, old-timer, I was taught better manners, but..." He grinned.

"You movin' on tonight?" Edwin asked, ignoring the old-timer comment. After all, it was true.

"Might be best. While we're not that close, I do know there may be those on the lookout for the new lawman. I don't want to cause you any problems," the young man grinned as he caught the look on Edwin's face.

Grinning, Edwin asked, "Like what?" He was curious, and if what he suspected was true, he wanted to know for sure, if that was possible.

"Well, let's just say those who are looking out for my arrival may have the idea that I shouldn't arrive. You know, they may try to stop me," he answered with a self-conscious grin.

"If we were to go together..." Edwin offered, thinking it might be safer to travel together. The young man stared at Edwin, thinking about the offer, then answered, "It's a good way to get hurt."

"Maybe, but I'm an old man. Don't think they would be expecting that. Could be safer for both of us."

The river flowed and sang its soothing song while Edwin waited for the young man's answer. Finally, he looked over at Edwin. He was trying to decide if he'd meant what he'd said about riding together despite the risk. With a shake of his head, the young man stuck out his hand. "Name's Taylor Wright, 'Tay' for short."

"Edwin Markham, but some have called me 'Win'," Edwin answered as he took the offered hand. "Now how about we get some rest and get an early start in the morning?"

Edwin banked the fire and was settling in when he heard a rustling just outside of camp. He looked over at Taylor, but the young man seemed unaffected by the noise. He was jumpy, and that didn't bode well for the rest of the journey or his state of mind.

"Relax, the horses will let us know if it's anything we need to worry about," Taylor said.

"Been a while since I slept out under the stars."

"You'll get used to it," Taylor assured the older man.

"Probably right," Edwin agreed as the rustling continued.

CHAPTER 4

Mary opened the store early despite — or because — she suffered a worried and restless night. She'd just finished sweeping the doorway when Agnes came striding up. "Mary, you realize what you've done?"

Of all the things to deal with early in the morning, listening to Agnes was not one she relished. Still, it was not in her to be rude, so she moved inside, allowing Agnes to precede her.

"Agnes, what are you referring to?"

Agnes followed Mary with her eyes as Mary moved behind the counter. Once Mary was set, Agnes started in. "That episode in the street. What were you thinking? I just felt it my duty to speak to you about it."

"Agnes, that man put a gun in a young boy's hand and wanted him to shoot."

"Many boys handle guns. We don't try to stop them, do we?"

Huffing out a breath, Mary patiently tried to explain. "Young Bobby had never held a gun before, you could tell by his reaction. Those who handle guns when young have been shown what to do. They have been taught what damage can occur when handled irresponsibly. Bobby knew none of that, and he could have killed someone. Think of how that would haunt him?"

"That doesn't mean you need to take it upon yourself to confront such..."

"Mary," Red, called as she strode into the store.

Mary took notice of the way Red moved, sober, her walk steady. It was a pleasant surprise, but what did she want? At least her arrival cut short Agnes and her tirade.

Red stood looking at Mary, curiosity, and patience in her smile, then her look slid to Agnes.

"What?" Mary asked in answer to Red's entrance.

"I must be going," Agnes sniffed, then turned and marched to the door, casting an *I'm better than thou* look at Red as she circled widely around the young woman. "We can continue this discussion later, Mrs. Gilpin, just remember what I said."

Mary cringed at Agnes' action, but Red took it in stride, moving away from the door to allow the older woman to pass.

"You're staring at me. Yes, I'm sober." Red laughed, then turned serious. "Mary, I needed to be sober so that you'd believe me when I told you, they are out to get you."

Mary grinned, then sobered herself. Red might be a plain-speaking young woman, but Mary preferred that. "What do you mean, out to get me?"

"I need you to believe me when I say you need to be wary."

Mary smiled, her tone gentle as she respond-ed, "Red, I'm always wary, but what do I need to be wary of?"

Red shook her head, "You don't understand, I heard Stu talking and—"

Mary placed her hand on the young woman's arm, "Red, I appreciate your concern, I do, but I won't change for anyone."

"You misunderstand," Red tried again, placing her hand over Mary's as she nodded toward the door. "It's like Stu can't let go of what you did to him yesterday. How can I say this? It's like there is water everywhere, but he can't drink it, he's too focused on this one thing."

Mary watched Red, saw the deep concern in her eyes. She'd always known deep down Red was a good person, despite the company she kept. Still, the effort she put in to help, made Mary admire her even more.

"Red, what you're doing means so much to me," Mary replied while reaching out to pull the young woman closer and hug her. "And I will be careful, but Stu cannot be allowed..." Mary stopped as Stu walked in. That he had been drinking was evident.

Red jerked back, but Stu grabbed her arm, pulling her even farther away from Mary. "Just what are you...?"

Quickly Mary moved, placing herself in front of Stu, "Not that it matters... "

"Damn right it don't," Stu snarled.

Mary continued, ignoring the interruption. "But Red came to tell me you are upset about yesterday."

Red shot a frightened look at Mary. Ignoring Red's reaction, she continued, finger pointed at Stu, "And I would do it again. And you know this if anything—even a small bruise—happens to Red, I'll..."

Stu lunged toward Mary, stopping just short of knocking her down with his body. Perhaps he expected Mary to react in fear and move away. Instead, Mary had not moved.

"Go back and sober up," Mary told him. "You were a fool yesterday, don't compound it by doing something even more stupid today."

"Why you," Stu sputtered, then raising his fist, he drew back, preparing to strike Mary, but his movement was cut short by a voice from the door.

"If you even move one inch toward either woman, it will be one of the last acts you'll do in this town," the smooth baritone voice said, halting Stu and startling the women.

Stu froze, his face blanching. Then the alcohol kicked in. "Where else would I go?" Stu asked, "I'm needed here."

The speaker, his white hair in stark contrast to the cold brown eyes and black brows, looked at Stu. Without any warning, the man knocked Stu down. No easy thing, considering Stu's size compared to the man. Placing a shined, booted foot on Stu's throat, the man smiled. As he looked down, he gently spoke, a whisper, "You will go nowhere."

Stu understood the threat all too well as he tried to fall deeper into the floor, all bravado was gone now.

Mary and Red watched in startled silence. They hadn't heard the threat, they only saw the man continue to put constant pressure on Stu's throat. Just when the watchers thought they would have to remove a dead man from the premises, the foot rose, and Stu coughed, trying to regain his breath.

"Now, get out of here and sober up."

Stu rose on all fours after first trying to stand. He crawled away, finally standing when he reached the door frame and pulled himself erect.

Mary started to speak when she was interrupted, "Young lady," the man said to Red, "I would like to speak to Mary alone."

Red started to protest, but Mary nodded and Red reluctantly walked out the door. There she paused, but the man made a shooing motion with his hand, so she scurried away.

"How did you know my name?" Mary asked the question foremost in her mind. That he knew her, while she knew nothing of him caused even more unease than her confrontation with Stu.

"I know a great deal about you," he replied.

Mary felt a flutter of nerves start in her stomach and spread out to her limbs. Her rescuer was not what he seemed.

The man smiled and with a slight nod of his head, continued, "My older brother always thought small, and did you a great disservice when he killed your husband. He only thought about the money in the bank."

Mary stared, "Your....? "

"Yes, my brother."

"Cornelius Stuart didn't have a brother, at least not one he spoke about," Mary stated.

"Well, perhaps I should say, step-brother. I'm Bill Thornton," the man bowed slightly. "We didn't always see eye to eye."

Mary had never seen such coldness in a person's eyes when talking of a relative, even one as tenuous as a stepbrother. Just watching him made her feel cold.

"But I must warn you," Thornton continued, "I've kept the men from harassing you, howev er..." he let the sentence hang.

Mary realized there was more she needed to know about this man. He seemed to be behind what was happening around here, Mary was sure. Still, despite his warning, she would not allow any of them to abuse the children. On that thought, she looked at Thornton, the brother of the man who'd ruined her life, saying, "Thank you, for your kindness. Know this, I will not allow actions, such as those of Stu's, to continue."

He smiled, "On that one thing we agree, for the moment." With a bow, he turned toward the door. There he stopped, turning his head, he added, "But move forward carefully." Then he was gone, but the threat hung in the air, and Mary took him at his word for now.

CHAPTER 5

As Edwin neared his destination, he imagined the reunion with Mary. Swaying with the rhythm of the horse's gait, the heat rising from the ground, none of this affected Edwin. He was so deep in his daydream of what was to come. He saw Mary, her auburn hair, her eyes smiling at the sight of him. He returned that smile, behind his closed eyes. He was taking in the beauty that was his memory of Mary.

"Hey, you asleep?" Taylor's voice cut in.

"No, I'm awake, just keeping my eyes safe from the heat and glare of the surroundings," Edwin quickly answered, eyes popping open. "Why anyone would want to live in this godforsaken place?" he mumbled. Now that the dream was gone, he forced himself to take in all of the lands that Mary now lived in.

"They say there's money to be made," Taylor replied. "This middle of nowhere, as folks like to say, and it is ripe for..."

"Ripe for what?" Edwin interrupted.

"We're heading to Booming," Taylor answered. "Someone must think there is money, or the town wouldn't be having the problems it seems to be having."

"You may be right. Hope my friend Mary is doing okay. That's why I'm heading down there." Edwin closed his eyes again, this time against the sun's glare, but the dream refused to return. He was worried about Mary, worried he wouldn't be able to help. It was the helpless feeling he wanted to deny, but it was there. Well, he'd just have to work through it.

"Who's this Mary?" Taylor asked. "A relative or..."

"She's someone I grew up with. Heard she had a store down there, and with the trouble, I thought maybe she'd like to leave. I just want to help," Edwin finished lamely.

The closer Edwin came to his destination, the more nervous he felt. What if Mary weren't there, or worse something had happened to her? She hadn't deserved the hand that life dealt her. Edwin felt guilty, for not being there to help her through. He cut his thoughts short. He'd enough of self-pity. He was doing what he could now, whatever that might be. But, what if she didn't want help? The thoughts and questions fought each other as Edwin moved closer to his destiny.

The two traveled in silence, each deep in their thoughts about what was to come. The miles drifted by, heat waves rolling off the ground as they slowly made their way through the high plains east of the mountains, barely visible off in the distance to the west.

Taylor watched Edwin. He was wondering what it was that was pushing the man toward trouble instead of away. He'd noticed that periodically Edwin would put his left hand in his pocket when it looked like he was worried.

He was curious but didn't want to intrude. Truth to tell, he was worried himself. As a deputy in Denver, he'd had his fair share of confrontations, but always had someone who would help out, even if it was some time in coming. He had people to back him up in court, and on the street after making an arrest. It had helped to have someone to talk over the cases and clues with. Where he was going, it would probably be just him. Even at the age of twenty-four, he had the experience, but would he be up to the challenge? Well, he would find out soon enough.

About one in the afternoon, as if by unspoken agreement, the two pulled up to a small wash with just a trickle of water. It had at least enough for the horses to quench their thirst.

The two were preparing to head out, for Booming was only a few hours away, when they heard the thunder of horses, heading toward them. They had agreed it might be better to not announce Taylor's real reason for being in the area until they knew what was going on.

"What you think they want?" Taylor asked as he tightened the cinch. He continued, "And looks like we'll find out soon, here they come."

The two waited next to their horses as a group of seven men rode up.

"Howdy," Edwin said as the group surrounded the two. Out of the corner of his eye, Edwin watched Taylor, noting the young man's hand casually moving toward his pistol. "Help you, gentlemen?"

"Yeah, you just might," the man in front answered. His features were dark and his small eyes were darting between Edwin and Taylor. "You see a young man riding this way?"

Caution, plus the look of the other men prompted Edwin to answer, "No, haven't seen anyone riding by. My friend and me, we're heading to Booming to visit a friend."

"Friend huh, maybe we know him, seein' as we're from around those parts."

"It's a her, a friend from childhood. She has a store there."

"You must mean Mary," the way the man said her name only increased Edwin's concern and the caution he'd felt earlier.

"That's her," Edwin said. "Is everything okay?"

"She's fine, ain't she boys?"

Edwin could only speculate what that might mean. Regardless, their reaction just firmed his resolve to arrive in Booming as soon as possible.

"That's good to know. By the way, this man you're looking for. He in trouble? Have a name?" Edwin inquired.

"No name, just a description. Looks a lot like your friend, except he's the new marshal. Might say we're the welcoming committee," The man answered with a laugh, followed by laughter from the rest. The sound of a devil's laugh.

Edwin had watched Taylor's eyes at the man's statement. Quickly he answered, "Well if we see this man, we'll let him know you're looking for him."

The speaker gave the two a hard look, then turning his horse, called to the others, "Let's go, boys," then to Edwin he said, "you have him look up Thornton when he gets to town."

"I'll let him know, should I see that lone rider," Edwin called as the group rode away.

When they were out of earshot, Taylor said, "When they find out you lied..."

"Taylor, I didn't lie. I just didn't tell them everything, and from the way they acted, I'd say we need to be careful and get to Booming as soon as possible. And when we get there, find out who this Thornton is."

CHAPTER 6

Mary's desire for sleep weighed heavily on her. It had been three days since her meeting with Bill Thornton. And those three nights she'd sat in her store, watching and thinking about the tension and fear growing outside her doors. She survived and was left alone, so far. Her business had not suffered as some had. That was surprising, but then perhaps not, considering her meeting with Thornton. Was it her willingness to stand up to the violence that had earned her some respect? Or perhaps it was because she was a woman? She didn't believe Thornton when he said he'd not let the others harm her due to a past wrong. She felt it was only a matter of time.

Mary rested only in the wee hours of the morning, after the bedlam, the fear of violence, had subsided. But she remained in the store proper, resting in her chair, shotgun across her lap. It was not the restful sleep she needed, but she didn't feel her store would be safe if she left to go to her rooms in the back.

It was in those early hours she let herself wish her life had been different. She allowed herself to think of a life with her husband if he were still alive. Thoughts of the life she'd have if the son she'd given up was still with her. Tears, long held in check would escape her eyes and trace rivers down her cheeks.

Last night had been the worst. Thoughts of her son, long held at bay, had come back into the carefully built life she'd been living. The pain she'd buried forced its way to the surface. What had become of him? Did he have a good upbringing? Had the people she'd been forced to leave him with love him like their own? Forcing herself to breathe, Mary worked to gather the threads of that shattered life back into the box she had kept them in and prepared to meet the day.

Mary wiped her eyes and started sweeping up. Thoughts of giving up and running away never occurred to her. She'd done that once and decreed it would never happen again.

With the jingle of the bell, Mary turned, a forced smile on her face.

"What can I do for you?" She asked the two silhouettes standing just inside the door, with the sun at their backs. Silence greeted her question, so she repeated it, just in case they hadn't heard the first time. The two walked out of the shadow and into the light from the sun shining through the window. Mary's throat closed, no sound would come as she took in the scene in front of her. It couldn't be.

Edwin stood watching Mary, her reaction to him and Taylor. *Why doesn't she say something?* Edwin wondered.

"Hello Mary," Edwin said into the growing silence. "I was in the area and thought I'd stop by and say hello."

Taylor stared at Edwin, for he knew otherwise, but at a glance from the man, he kept his thoughts to himself. There was something else going on here, and he wanted to see where it led.

"Edwin?"

Edwin could hear the question in Mary's voice. He didn't think he'd changed that much, just a few wrinkles and gray hair. Mary's response puzzled him. It was almost like she was upset or worried that he was here. He knew things were uneasy, but why would that make any difference?

"Yep, it's me," Edwin answered, removing his hat, a self-effacing grin on his face.

Silence greeted Edwin's words. "And this is Taylor." He didn't add that Taylor was the new marshal, for they'd agreed to keep that quiet until they knew more about what was happening in the town.

"Pleased to meet you, ma'am," Taylor said as he doffed his hat and smiled.

Mary shook herself and moving forward gave Edwin a hug, which brought a sigh of relief from him as he began, "I was beginning to think you..."

"Edwin, so sorry. All the people to walk through that door, I never expected to see you."

Edwin moved Mary back to arms-length, a true grin on his face. He placed gentle hands on her shoulders.

"Edwin, why are you here?" Mary asked. Although seeing him brought back memories, both happy and sad, she feared what might happen to him. "And why did you bring your son?"

Of all the responses, this was so unexpected. Edwin shook his head. "Mary, Taylor's not my son. We met on the trail."

He was not wanting to judge, but from Mary's reaction, it seemed he'd made the trip for nothing. He hadn't anticipated she would run to him, like a long-lost love; well maybe he had, but there was a restraint to Mary that made Edwin uneasy.

Through the whole exchange between the two, Taylor had watched, his face a study as he observed the interaction between the two.

"Edwin, you misunderstand. I'm glad to see you, but with all the things that's been happening..." Mary shrugged her shoulders.

Reaching for Mary's hands, Edwin smiled as he said, "Mary, that's why I'm here I want to help."

"Oh Edwin, ever the gallant friend," Mary laughed, but there was a sadness in her eyes as she withdrew her hands from Edwin's.

With the removal of Mary's hands, Edwin's left hand went to his pocket, thumb rubbing the locket. He hadn't expected Mary to praise and start kissing him. He was too old and realistic for that, but it hurt that she didn't take him seriously. It was crushing that she still saw him like some fool who would rush in for no reason.

"Ma'am," Taylor said into the silence that had grown between the two.

"Please call me Mary," she said as she smiled at Taylor.

"Mary," Taylor bowed, "I'll leave you two to catch up. Edwin meet you later at the livery? While I'm at it, I'll take your horse over with mine."

"Sure, and thanks."

"Come by again," Mary called after Taylor. She looked at Edwin and the silence grew until it was obvious that an awkwardness existed between them.

Why, why, why, did I think I could waltz in as if nothing had happened, thrummed through Edwin's mind. He'd been a fool. Well, if he could, he'd do what he could to help Taylor as long as he didn't have to hurt anyone. He'd had enough of that in the war. Still, even though Mary seemed distant, the town and surrounding area needed help. He decided since he was here, the trip needn't be a waste. Besides, he just might get lucky and Mary would change her mind about his being here. He gave Mary a sad smile, saying, "It was good to see you. I'll go help, Taylor."

He'd just stepped on the boardwalk outside the store when he heard footsteps behind him.

"Edwin," Mary's voice reached his ears. "Stay."

A contrariness rose and Edwin heard himself say, "Don't want to interfere," while he cursed himself for being a fool the minute the words were said.

"None of that," Mary ordered, and with a firm but gentle hand brought Edwin back into the store.

"Let's start over," Mary smiled, pulling another chair close to the one behind the counter. "I am happy to see you. It's been so many years and a lot of miles from Lee County, Iowa. Come, sit down," she suggested, patting the seat of the chair beside her.

Edwin, although uncomfortable, took the chair Mary had moved for him to sit in.

Searching for something to say, Edwin finally said, "It has been a long time. Funny thing is, I only live about ninety miles away," Edwin finished, trying to sound casual, but realized now he was here next to Mary, all the things he thought he'd say just didn't seem to work. Yes, it was Mary, just as beautiful as ever, but also an older and stronger Mary. Edwin didn't know where he could fit in with the life she created for herself. Still, he could offer her his friendship. He hoped that would never change.

"So how did you know where I was?" Mary asked, interrupting Edwin's thoughts.

"Chet stopped by Kiowa Wells, and he mentioned he'd seen you," Edwin didn't feel he needed to tell Mary the whole story. He was embarrassed at how violent he'd become when he'd heard she might be in trouble.

"Chet? I don't recall seeing him here."

The look of concern in Mary's eyes prompted Edwin to say, "Don't know about that, but he said he'd seen you." The question also made Edwin wonder how Chet knew Mary was here. He supposed Chet could have been riding through and seen Mary without her having seen him, but he was under the impression Chet had been around the area, more than just a casual ride through. If that was the case, what reason would he have for being here? Or for that matter, what brought him to such a small town like Kiowa Wells? In his haste to get to Mary, he'd not only gotten himself run down by a horse and clipped by its hoof but he may also have been sought out. But why?

The two were interrupted when Red walked in. "Mary," she started, then seeing Edwin continued, "sorry to intrude."

"That's okay, Red, this is an old friend. We were just catching up."

Offering her hand to Edwin, who had risen at her entrance, Red said, "They call me Red."

Taking the hand, and bringing it to his lips, said, "Pleased to meet you Red, I'm Edwin."

"Oh Mary, they must have taught them good where you came from."

Mary smiled at the two, and shaking her finger at Edwin, "Don't let him fool you."

"I'm hurt to the quick," Edwin said, then nodding to the two women headed out the door. "Pleasure to meet you Red. Mary, I'll be back later and we can finish catching up."

CHAPTER 7

Taylor left Edwin and Mary to get reacquainted. He smiled to himself. The meeting wasn't as sweet as he thought Edwin wanted it to be. Taylor thought it was funny that Mary believed he was Edwin's son.

On the way to the livery, Taylor noticed there was more to the town than he thought. He stabled the horses and headed out to survey the community. He turned left out the door walking on the north side of the street. He'd noticed when he and Edwin arrived, there were two main streets. There were regular businesses on the street he now walked, and if the noise were any indication, the rowdy businesses were on the street to the south. The homes were spread out around the edges. For a new town on the edge of the border, it was larger than he'd expected.

He could smell old smoke, a charcoal smell of burnt buildings. He also noticed a few empty lots where buildings had once stood, and nothing had been rebuilt yet. Some lots had new lumber nearby, others housed empty shells.

At one of the empty lots, he reached down to pick up a charred sign. What words he could make out were 'gold', 'silver', and what looked like the word 'Dragon'. Looking at the shell of the building, and some of the other lots, he thought it looked like a dragon had been through the area. Thinking about dragons brought a smile to his face. He guessed he'd rather face a dragon-like the knights of yore, than the group that was responsible for his being sent here.

Crossing the street, Taylor wandered over to South Street. He was greeted with a cacophony of shouts, pianos playing different tunes along with a lot of off-key singing. He couldn't remember when "Danny boy" had sounded like a military march.

He found a small, fairly quiet place and entered. The sign said 'Micah's Place'. He moved to the bar, and when the bartender moved his way, Taylor asked if they carried cider.

"We have some of the best around, make it myself," the man behind the bar beamed.

"Then I'll give it a try."

"Don't know why most folks don't drink it. Seems most would want to give it a try," the man said as he placed the drink in front of Taylor.

Taking a sip, Taylor struggled to not cough. Instead of the smooth bite of cider that he was expecting, this drink tasted like someone had poured a bunch of hot chili peppers in it. Fortunately, the second sip went down easier. With the lift of an eyebrow, Taylor nodded to the drink, "You do have a way with cider."

With a huge grin, the man offered his hand. "Name's Micah or Mike for short. Not many can handle more than one sip. I'm impressed."

"You have to tell me your secret sometime," Taylor said as he took the offered hand. "You can call me Taylor or Tay for short."

"Glad to meet you, Tay."

Taylor could tell the man had more questions but was wise enough not to step over that line. Micah wanted to know but wasn't going to be intrusive. He wondered if it was natural with Micah or something he'd learn to survive in his business. Or perhaps it was a reaction to what was happening? Either way, the fact that he was surviving was what mattered, Taylor supposed. He liked the man, but wondered if he was one of the good guys or not.

"Same here." Taylor grinned. "Nice place, and if I may ask, what caused the fires I noticed? They seemed to be a hit and miss affair."

The bartender paused, looking around. He'd started to answer when a couple of men walked in.

Taylor watched as the bartender's eyes narrowed. Then the man moved down the bar to take care of the two.

They glanced at Taylor, taking in his young appearance and lack of a weapon. Something Taylor had decided might be the safest way to approach the town and its residents. Now, looking at these two, he was beginning to doubt that choice.

"Kinda naked ain't ya?" The shorter man asked, his eyes on Taylor.

The bartender shot Taylor a warning look, as if to say, here was danger and tread carefully.

"Just arrived," Taylor answered, "didn't want to give the wrong impression."

"Smart, maybe too smart," the man said.

The other leaned over and whispered in the short man's ear. Then the two turned to Taylor, the other asking, "You come in with that older feller?"

Taylor nodded. He watched the two carefully. There was something not quite right about the situation. He wondered if he was catching a break, providing he made it out of the place intact.

"He a lawman?"

Now Micah looked deeply worried. He had taken a liking to this young man and would hate to see him meet his end so quickly, and for so small a reason.

"No, he just came in to see an old friend he used to know."

"Well, you tell him to watch out. Seems I saw him with Mary and she's a troublemaker." The short man warned although the look in his eye said the warning was just something he was supposed to say.

Lifting his drink in salute to the two, Taylor said, "I'll pass it on." Then he drained the glass and set it back on the bar. He exhaled, stifling the look of pain from showing on his face.

"Did you see that?" The tall man asked, awe in his voice.

"Don't believe it, even though I saw it," Shorty said, then turning to Micah asked, "that the real thing?"

"Of course."

"I'll be... You do beat all, young feller, they call me Shorty," Shorty said, awe in his voice. "Any man that can swallow that drink whole, well, you're more of a man than I thought. Ain't he?" Shorty asked his partner

"Yeah, sure. We gotta..." the tall one began, turning to Micah.

Taylor watched as Micah pulled out some cash from the drawer, then handed it to the man.

"Mr. Thornton thanks you for your generosity," Shorty grinned. "See you around young fella," as he and the taller man downed the drinks they hadn't paid for and left.

Taylor watched the two leave, then looked at Micah. "That why you survive?" Taylor offered.

"May not like it, but it's the price of doing business." Micah grinned a sad grin, "And Shorty isn't as bad as Alver, the tall one. That man seems to enjoy the rougher part of his job."

"Good thing to know. Thanks," Taylor said, then continued, "guess it makes sense to keep the powers that be happy, long as it doesn't catch up to you in the end." Taylor found himself wondering if Mary also paid for protection. Somehow he couldn't see her doing that. Still?

Micah sighed his agreement, then he grinned, "Want another cider?"

"Don't think I'd survive more'n one," Taylor grinned, "You'd started to tell me about the fires, they have anything to do with what I saw today?"

Micah nodded. "Stop by again and maybe we can talk. Should be another week before I have my visitors again."

"Will do," Taylor said, dropping his payment on the bar. With a wave to Micah, Taylor headed over to the livery to meet Edwin. He grinned, wondering how the rest of the reunion had gone.

CHAPTER 8

The next day found Edwin in the storeroom digging into Mary's supplies, what was left of them. Each time the bell over the door rang, he argued with himself. He knew Mary was an independent woman, he loved that new aspect about her, but she was taking on more than one person should handle. Yet every time he took a step to go help, he stopped. It seemed better to just be a friend. Then when he proposed – well he didn't want to think of that.

The bell rang again, followed by a shout to "lookout" as a gunshot rang out. Dropping the box of biscuits he'd been sorting, Edwin dashed to the front of the store. He stopped just shy of entering the store portion of the building. Mary stood behind the counter, shotgun pointed right at a young man, swaying with a pistol in his hand.

"Unless you can behave, you and the gun you have in your hand can just leave," Mary ordered.

"But, I just wanted to..."

"You do not come in my store drunk and shooting a weapon," Mary said, then continued, "if there is any shooting to be done, I'll do it."

"Didn't mean..." the young man mumbled as he staggered out the door, running into Agnes as he left.

Agnes glared at the young man, then, looking in at Mary, she sniffed and continued down the street.

Glancing over and seeing Edwin, Mary smiled and with a sigh, placed the shotgun within easy reach under the counter.

"Why don't we both take a break?" Mary asked.

Edwin wanted to question Mary about what just happened. However, he felt it might be better to let Mary tell it in her own time. Instead, he smiled, and wiping his hands on his pants, confessed, "I have some biscuits to pick up. The shot surprised me."

"That can wait," Mary said as she locked the doors to the store. She pulled Edwin back toward her living quarters. There she indicated the table and chairs. "Right now, I just want to sit, relax, and maybe catch up with what you've been doing the last twenty plus years."

Edwin and Mary did just that. The hours sped by in pleasant reminiscence of the intervening years. Mary, Edwin noticed, avoided anything about their former relationship. For himself, Edwin didn't ask anything about how she ended up in such a place as this. The two soon noticed the stars were beginning their journey across the sky.

"I made some cookies the other day, would you like one?" Mary asked as the conversation began to lag with the coming of evening.

"That would be nice, although I don't remember you doing much cooking or baking," Edwin joked. Then, seeing the look in Mary's eye he added, "I'm sure they'd be mighty good. While you get the cookies, I'll just go take care of those biscuits."

Edwin followed Mary to the front. As he turned the corner he saw Mary, who had walked to the front window, staring out. The leaves were dancing across the street, the wind playing the tune, but she didn't seem to notice them. Her face had turned white, her eyes were large and fearful.

"What's wrong?" Edwin questioned as he moved toward Mary. The closer he moved toward her, the more horrified he became. Outside a body was swinging in time with the wind, first, a glimpse then back to the black night. With a curse Edwin started for the door, asking, "Do you recognize him?"

"He was a homesteader who just started working a small place outside of town," Mary sobbed. "I remember he came in during a thunderstorm looking to order trees to be delivered. He'd hoped to make a new start with his son and the son's wife and child."

Edwin cut the man down. As he maneuvered the corpse through the door, the bell above it kept clanging with the wind. He'd just finished and shut the door, when two men, one short, the other tall, came in.

"Whoever cut down the trespasser made a mistake. If we'd wanted him down, we'd have taken care of it," the tall one said.

Such a cavalier attitude had both Edwin and Mary seething.

"Well, he's down now, and we'll take care of the body," Edwin said.

"Is that so?"

"Yes, it is, Alver," Mary replied, her answer backed up by the shotgun in her hands.

"Thornton ain't gonna like..."

"You can tell Mr. Thornton I don't appreciate bodies hanging outside my store," Mary interrupted. "Now, leave." She enforced that statement with the waving of the shotgun.

As the two departed, Edwin bent down to check the body. He found the man had been dead before he'd been placed outside the store. Someone had shot him in the back. Edwin checked the pockets. In one he found a list of people, people he'd known in the Army. Looking closer at the body, he realized the dead man was Joe Logan, a man he'd served with. The list, which contained his name, worried him. Not only was he trying to help Mary and Taylor, now it looked like he needed to do some digging into his past. Problem was, he didn't know where to start.

Seeing Edwin's frown, Mary asked, "What is it?"

Putting the list in his pocket as he rose, Edwin shrugged, "I was startled. His name was Joe, I knew him back in the war. Why don't you go get some rest? I'll have Taylor help me take Joe's body out of here."

Mary wanted to argue, but she was tired. She was worried about Edwin's reaction, but he had closed himself off. With a sad smile, Mary walked up and placed a kiss on Edwin's cheek, "I'll go make some coffee. Come back when you finish."

"Mary," Edwin interrupted concern for her showing in his eyes.

Mary responded with a slight grin, "Then I'll go get some sleep after I lock up. You better get going."

CHAPTER 9

The store was in shadow as the sun started over the horizon. Slowly, the light drove the darkness farther back. Mary came from her living quarters, feeling rested for the first time in days. She moved to the front, intent on checking for any damage that might have occurred during the night.

A slight breeze blew puffs of dust down the street. Mary enjoyed the early mornings as the sun shone on a new day. Perhaps it was just wishful thinking, but mornings gave her hope. She was surprised to see Edwin coming up the street. A picture of him doing the same thing all those years ago overlay the present. She started to frown, followed quickly by a smile. Edwin had only been in town for two days, and here she was acting like the young girl she'd been before life got in the way.

The ringing of the bell above the door brought a grinning Edwin inside. At the sight of Mary, his eyes glowed. "You're just like the picture I've kept in my head of you," he said, reaching to pull her close.

Mary relaxed into the safety Edwin's arms offered. The years fell away, and she was the young girl who had believed in a happy ever after, and the gift of friends. A weight lifted from her heart and mind, if only for a brief time.

Emboldened by Mary's reaction, Edwin blurted out, "Mary, come back to Kiowa Wells with me, let me take care of you," his chin resting against the hair at the top of her head. "You needn't work or have to worry anymore."

Pulling back, Mary shot Edwin a look. Moving away, she kept her face averted, not wanting Edwin to see the pain in her eyes. Even as Edwin reached out for her, she evaded his tender hands. *Never again would she put her faith in the words of another,* Mary thought, it was just too dangerous and painful. Her freedom and self-sufficiency, she would not give up, not for anything. She couldn't handle the pain of loss again.

"Mary?" She heard the question that was in Edwin's voice. She had hurt him, but better now than later. He would get over it, realize it wasn't meant to be. They'd do best to remain friends.

"It's nothing," Mary lied. "I'd best get ready for whatever fresh hell may show up today."

Before Edwin could reply, the bell rang as the door swung open. A young man came striding in, walking straight toward Mary.

"Mary," the young man began, "I understand there was a corpse hanging outside your door, but when I asked about it..."

"Edwin cut it down last night."

"Edwin?" The young man questioned.

Pointing in Edwin's direction, Mary continued, "He and his friend Taylor took care of it last night."

Edwin didn't hear the question or answer. The sight of the young man took him back to a cold, rainy day in late November, back to the camp at Pacific City in Missouri. There had been an outbreak of measles, and many of the Iowa Light Infantry had contracted the disease. He'd been on guard when a scouting expedition had returned from checking the area of a nearby destroyed rebel base. The town and surrounding area had been burned and the rebels were driven away. Joe Logan had looked scared and seemed to try to avoid the others who had been with him. This young man looked just like Joe.

"Edwin?" Mary queried. "This young man was asking about the man...," she stopped when Edwin looked at her.

"Yes?" Edwin began, finally getting over the shock of seeing the young man standing in the store. Still staring, Edwin said, "Joe?"

"Yes, that was my father's name, I'm Joe junior," the young man answered. "Folks always call me Junior."

"Edwin, was there any problem with the corpse?" Mary interrupted.

Both men turned, "What?" Edwin asked.

"Was there a problem with the undertaker or any of the others?"

Edwin caught the look of fear in Mary's eyes. The young man glanced from one to the other, trying to read the signals the two were sharing.

"Was there trouble last night? Why would...?" Edwin began before Mary cut in.

"Remember, someone took exception to our cutting the man down," Mary answered.

"No, there was no trouble," Edwin assured her as he turned back to Junior.

"Did you know him?" Junior asked.

"I'd met your father during the war," Edwin told Junior.

"We're new to this area," Junior began. "After my mother died, back in Illinois, Pa said we should start new. We hoped to earn the land by growing trees with the Timber Culture act. I think he was afraid of something, but he never said anything. Now, this happens." Junior shook himself, like trying to shake off a bad dream.

Edwin wanted to ask more questions about what Joe might have been afraid of, but not in front of Mary. "How about I go with you to take a look at the body?"

Junior looked relieved as he answered, "I'd appreciate that."

"You be careful, both of you. I don't want you to end up in more trouble," Mary ordered as the two exited the store. Mary sent a prayer after them, knowing they'd need all the help they could get.

"So, you knew my pa in the war?" Junior asked as the two men headed over to where Edwin and Taylor had taken the body last night.

"We were in Missouri together early on," Edwin answered. "Did he do okay after?"

Junior thought for a moment, "We did okay, but after Ma died, well actually over the last year, he seemed jumpy. I tried to ask him why he was so jumpy. He told me it was nothing."

The answer did nothing to calm Edwin's concerns, but Junior's next words helped some.

"I figure it was someone else who was upset that they'd been forced off their grazing range."

"Why do you say that?" Edwin asked, but knew that when areas of rangeland were opened for settlement, there were problems. The town and area he'd come from had worked it out, but a lot of places weren't that lucky.

Junior's eyes grew hard, "There were three men who cornered Pa about sundown a few weeks back and were pushing him around. Don't know what would've happened if I hadn't stepped out with the rifle."

"Any idea who it may have been?"

"It was dark, and they took off. The funny thing was Pa wouldn't talk about it."

Edwin saw Taylor approaching, and waving him over, introduced Junior.

"Taylor, this is Joe 'Junior' Logan, the lynched man's son."

Junior offered his hand and Taylor shook it, "Pleasure to meet you, but not under these circumstances."

"We were headed over so Junior could take the body back home. I would like to get back to Mary's. Do you mind taking Junior the rest of the way?" Edwin asked.

"Sure."

"Thanks for all you've done." Junior shook Edwin's hand.

"You plan on staying around?" Edwin inquired of Junior.

Shaking his head, Junior answered, "I have a wife who's expecting and a two-year-old son. He thought the world of his grandfather. I think once this is all settled we will head farther west, push on toward Trinidad. Might be best for the whole family."

"Well, I wish you the best. Taylor here or I can help if you need anything."

"Thanks again," Junior said as he and Taylor continued to where Joe's body was, while Edwin made his way back to Mary's.

"Okay Edwin, you seemed to recognize that young man. What's going on here?" Mary asked, hands across her stomach as Edwin walked in.

Despite the store being empty, Mary's interrogation put Edwin on the defensive. His life and his past were his own, but were they? Why did death always rear its head to ruin what was good? He'd felt that way during the war, and now here it was again.

Edwin sighed, then shrugged his shoulders. It wouldn't help anything being angry. With eyes that mirrored resignation, he turned, "He looked like a man I knew in the war, the man who was hanging outside your store."

"Why didn't you tell me?" Mary questioned.

"I didn't think it was anything," Edwin answered shaking his head. "It was just a part of the past I've tried to leave behind. I did my duty in the war, but I wanted, and still want, to leave that in the past, where it belongs."

"But Edwin, you can't run away."

"Mary, that was over twenty years ago." Edwin sighed, closing his eyes, yet seeing that cold Missouri night again.

"So, you're going to go on ignoring it, but I can tell it still bothers you a lot," Mary said as she grabbed Edwin's shoulders, giving them a shake. "It's a part of who you are if you keep hiding from it..."

"What do you know of it?" Edwin growled.

The sun had passed its zenith and shadows were slowly overtaking what light there was in the store. It reflected Edwin's thoughts as he stared at the woman he'd loved and admired all these years. Why did she have to prod, to stubbornly bring up war and then demand he let it be? What did she know?

"If you ask me, you are just plain scared," Mary said. "As long as you continue to beat yourself up, you won't get over whatever is bothering you."

"Mary," Edwin gritted out. The fire in his eyes was nothing compared to the power of the pain he was feeling in his heart. "How dare you jud ge..." he ground out.

Mary stared at Edwin, frustrated, and ready to make him see sense, but the bell signaled the arrival of Red. She was sober and dressed conservatively.

"Is Mary in?" Red asked, looking around but she didn't see Mary standing behind Edwin.

"She's right here," Edwin replied as he moved aside so Red could see.

"What is it, Red"

The silence stretched as Red swayed back and forth, eyes looking anywhere but at Edwin and Mary. For his part, Edwin was trying to figure out what he should do next, while Mary waited patiently for Red to tell her why she'd come in. Edwin just couldn't shake the feeling something wasn't right when an explosion shook the building. The concussion knocked cans and dishes from their shelves. Red turned several shades whiter while Edwin started toward the rear of the store, intent on sneaking out and trying to pinpoint where the blast had been and, if possible, locate the perpetrators.

CHAPTER 10

Mary felt she should be more upset than she was because of the dead man. That she wasn't may have been in part due to Edwin being near, despite their recent quarrel. It was pleasant to share the burden, but then if life continued on the path her life had taken, Edwin would be lost to her also. The explosion last night nailed that thought. Mary wasn't sure she could handle losing another person who was so dear to her.

So involved in her thoughts, Mary missed Red as she staggered across the street, the 'good' people of the town averting their eyes. Only when the door opened, and Red fell through the door did Mary notice. She immediately moved to help Red up. She could tell the young woman was in shock, so different from the night before. Helping her to a chair, Mary went to the back to get supplies to treat the bruises on Red's arm. When she returned she asked, "Want to tell me what happened?" Although Mary suspected, she wanted to let Red tell her own story.

"We were playing, and things got a bit rough," Red answered, tentatively touching the growing purple bruise on her arm, avoiding Mary's eyes when she spoke. When Red saw no broken skin, she looked up at Mary, a guilty smile on her face. "I seem to have made a mess of things."

"It does happen," Mary said, placing a cool cloth over the injured area. *How true that is* Mary thought, her own life a prime example.

"Yes, it does," Red whispered, her eyes downcast once more.

Mary nodded and went back straightening an already straight store, giving Red time to relax, and perhaps eventually tell her the whole story.

Thinking about Red, she wondered yet again how this young girl, a pretty one at that, had gotten mixed up with such people. Mary thought a lot of Red and hoped she could help her in some way. She didn't like interfering in the lives of others, but she just couldn't stand by and do nothing to help. She had already challenged the powers in the town, what was one more added to the list?

Shaking her head, she turned back toward Red, asking, "You don't have to answer, but do you like your life?"

Red opened her eyes wide, glancing about as if to check that no one was listening. Finding no one, she still hesitated, a pain showing that had nothing to do with the bruises on her body.

"Don't worry, I won't tell anyone," Mary soothed. "But if you don't want..."

"Mary, it's not that, it's just..." Red sighed, a sad smile on her face, "what if they..."

"Red, if you wish, you can live in fear the rest of your life, but somehow I don't think that's what you want."

"If you are thinking of trying to help, they will come after you, last night's explosion was just a warning to you and the town," Red said. "I don't think I could live if anything happened to you."

Mary smiled, moving over to place an arm around Red's shoulders. "Don't worry about me. I've taken on such as this before. Besides, I have help."

"I don't know, I don't feel right about involving you," Red said, her voice falling to an almost inaudible whisper, her shoulders slumping, chin down to her chest.

Squeezing Red's shoulders, Mary said, "I understand, but if you ever need to talk or decide you want out, I'm here."

Red looked at Mary, giving her a wan smile. She rose as she said, "I'd better get back." She was walking out when Edwin and Taylor walked in.

Edwin noticed the look in Mary's eyes, while Taylor frowned as he noticed the bruises on the young woman's arm. Before Red walked out, Mary made introductions. "Red, you remember my old friend Edwin. The handsome young man is Taylor. Taylor, this is Red."

Red smiled at Edwin and blushed when she looked at Taylor. "Pleasure to meet you. Please don't think me rude, but I need to get back to work."

"May I have the pleasure of escorting you back?" Taylor asked, removing his hat and bowing.

Red looked at Mary, confusion on her face. Mary sensed the young woman was, for the first time, embarrassed about where she worked. With a smile, Mary nodded. With a self-conscious smile, Red offered her elbow to Taylor.

The two left, and Red was overheard saying, "I work at Thornton's saloon."

Taylor's voice carried to the two standing in the store, "Must be interesting..."

"I just stopped by to see if you'd like to join me for dinner," Edwin said, looking at the two as they moved across the street, Taylor holding protectively to Red's arm. He looked at Mary, awaiting her answer. Sensing she had other things on her mind, Edwin added, "We can talk about it then."

"I think that would be lovely. See you about five?" Mary answered, holding her arms across her waist.

"See you then, Mary," and with a wave, he headed out behind Taylor and Red.

When Edwin left, the sadness Mary felt at Red's situation drove her to a cleaning frenzy. Frustration at the situation here in town, Red and all the others, whirled round and round as Mary dusted, swept, and rearranged the store interior. She kept at it, with periodic breaks to help customers.

Finally, exhaustion and evening slowed Mary's steps. She pulled up the chair behind the counter and sat down. The feelings she'd been holding at bay bubbled up as the tears, tears that tracked from the corner of her eyes, only to be caught by her hand before they reached her cheeks.

Edwin walked in, and seeing Mary wiping her eyes, rushed over, pulling her up into a strong embrace. "What's wrong?" He asked, his chin resting on the top of Mary's head.

"I just..." She said into his shoulder, pausing, then looking up she continued, "is there no piercing this darkness that is casting a shadow over everything?"

"Mary, have faith, we will get through this," Edwin answered. Then taking a deep breath, he continued "You could marry me, and..." he hesitantly began.

Before he could finish, Mary reached up, placing her hand on his lips. "Don't."

Edwin looked down at Mary, her eyes serious. He'd taken a chance, but it seemed she didn't feel about him as he felt about her.

Taking her hand, he smiled, "Just offering a suggestion." With the squeeze of his fingers, Edwin turned and noting for the first time the state of the store, said, "You've been busy, but it's time for dinner."

Grabbing her shawl, Mary locked up as she and Edwin headed out to dinner. Edwin, with a smile on his face, started telling Mary about Red and Taylor and what happened when they arrived at Red's place of employment.

CHAPTER 11

As Mary and Edwin relaxed over coffee after a meal of steak and vegetables, the two fell into a companionable silence. They could hear the other patrons talking about the weather, about their children. The waitress came by to see if they needed more coffee, smiling as she refilled their cups, then asked if they would enjoy some dessert.

"What do you have?" Edwin asked.

"Cook made some cider cake today."

"Cider cake?" Mary looked puzzled. "I've not heard of that."

"Would you like to try a piece?" Edwin asked. "I think it sounds pretty good. Of course, I always did like cider," he finished with a smile.

Mary nodded, and soon there were two pieces of delicious cake sitting in front of them.

Sitting back after finishing, Mary smiled. "That was good."

"It was."

"Think the cook would share the recipe?"

"The worst you'd get is a no," Edwin grinned.

Mary called the waitress over. "Would the cook be willing to share the recipe? The cake was wonderful."

"I'll ask," the waitress grinned and headed back to the kitchen.

After the waitress left, Mary asked Edwin, "Edwin, what happened..."

"How do you mean?" Edwin frowned, although he thought he knew where the conversation might be heading.

"How did so many years and miles," Mary stopped then restarted. "Would you tell me why you left for the war? Why you didn't tell anyone you were going?"

Edwin stared into his coffee, wondering how he could answer that, especially since he'd regretted it early in the enlistment. He wanted to be truthful, but many didn't understand his reluctance to talk about the glory of battle. He didn't want to relive the things they'd been ordered to do. He still shuddered at the illness, the mud, the blood, and the... he stopped himself. He didn't want to remember that.

The silence grew as Mary wondered if she'd asked too much. She did want to know, and truly why Edwin had come all this way on the rumor that she might be in danger. If it was what she thought, then things might get uncomfortable. Still, she valued the friendship she'd had with Edwin and wanted to keep that.

Finally, Edwin looked up from his coffee and into Mary's eyes. "I almost wish I hadn't. It wasn't what I thought, and the things we did..."

Mary reached over, placing her hand over Edwin's as his words faded away. The sounds of the other patrons receded while the clock's ticking grew louder. Mary watched as Edwin seemed to fold in on himself, drawing away from the present to someplace in the past. She wondered if he even remembered she was there.

"I believed in keeping the country together, and allowing every man, woman, and child, no matter their color or status, to have a chance at following their dream. On that matter I'm still clear, as long as they don't step on or take advantage of others in following that dream,"

Edwin said, his mind still back in the past, in that time when he followed the others to war.

"If it's too painful," Mary began, her hand squeezing the strong forearm under it.

"No, it's just not something I've had anyone ask, or even care about for that matter," Edwin continued, "but then I've never been one to go around telling folks about those days either."

"Are the memories all bad?" The concern and sympathy in her voice came through as Edwin continued reliving those days in his mind.

Shaking his head, he answered, "No, I've some fond memories. I resolved to volunteer after I heard of the defeat at Manassas, I left at the first possible moment and signed up. I believed in the country staying together. I went to Dubuque and enlisted." Edwin paused, collecting his thoughts, and trying to decide what stories to tell Mary.

Mary remained quiet, hearing for the first time how Edwin, her dear childhood friend, became the man before her now.

Edwin started talking again. "We were to stay at Camp Worthington for some time, but on a September morning we got orders that we were to prepare for marching on a moment's notice." He smiled as he remembered how everyone was trying to figure out what was going to happen. "Some of the men thought we were going to be sent to Washington to reinforce the troops there. Others thought we were going to St. Louis. One private was very vocal about our going to Boonville via Patagonia. He just knew we were heading to a rebel battery a few miles below on either side of the river, that we were being sent to our deaths."

Mary, who'd been trying to visualize what Edwin was describing, caught her breath at the story unfolding before her. She'd not thought about what it might have been like. She knew her troubles were severe, but to face death and killing so frequently, what it must have done to Edwin. Her heart went out to him as he continued.

"The early days were filled with reveille at three o'clock in the morning. It was up to eat a hasty breakfast, strike our tents, shoulder our knapsacks, and go to wherever they ordered us to go. One time we were taking a horse and carriage from a couple of strong-minded ladies..."

What Edwin might have said was lost when Thornton's men came in. Mary caught her breath and her lips thinned, causing Edwin to look in the direction of her gaze. The three,

Shorty and two others, walked over to the waitress. Shorty grabbed her, trying to kiss her. Despite her efforts to push the man away, she was unsuccessful. Mary started to rise, but Edwin detained her, rising instead. He approached the three saying, "I think the lady doesn't want to be kissed."

"Listen, old man, this ain't none of your concern," the tall man said.

"Yeah, old man," the younger one added.

"Oh, come on, let it go. Can't you see this man's with Mary, and you know our orders," Shorty told the other two. "I didn't mean nothin' by it, Susanna here just brings out the lover in me, ain't that right?"

Edwin glanced at the waitress, who gave him a wan smile. "I think you might want to be more respectful in the future," Edwin advised.

"Anything you say," Shorty said. "Come on you two, we got other places to be."

Shorty smiled and nodded to Mary, and gave Susanna a look. "Be seein' you, later," he directed to Edwin.

Edwin placed an arm around Susanna's shoulder, asking, "You okay?"

"Sure, it happens sometimes, but usually nothing else," she whispered.

"If you're sure."

"I'm fine. Thank you."

Edwin returned to the table to find Mary glaring at him. "What's wrong?"

"How could you? Now you're a target. They wouldn't do anything to me, but you had to be the hero and look at what it's got you?" Mary blurted, grabbing her shawl and heading for the door.

Edwin quickly paid the bill and followed. "Mary, wait."

"I've nothing to say to you. Please leave me alone," Mary cried.

She was so upset and scared for Edwin. How like him to jump in without thinking. She couldn't lose her friend after finding him. *Men*, she thought, *can do the stupidest things.*

"Mary," Edwin called again, "at least let me make sure you make it home okay."

"Follow if you like, but I'll be fine."

"Mary, please consider leaving here and coming back home with me," Edwin called softly, moving close to Mary.

"Edwin, I had a lovely dinner, but you don't need to keep trying to save me. I've done fine so far and I'm not going to leave. Please, just go away and leave me alone," she said and hurried on.

Edwin followed, making sure she was safe, then, turning, made his way to where he and Taylor were staying. He didn't understand how Mary could be so angry. Well, he decided to sleep on it and try to get to the bottom of her reaction tomorrow. Maybe he could check and see if the cook decided to share the recipe for cider cake. It might help smooth things over.

CHAPTER 12

Edwin didn't go back to Mary's the next day. He decided instead to go with Junior as they took his father's body to the rail station after the town undertaker had prepared the body. They stopped off at Junior's house, where Edwin met Nettie, Junior's wife.

"I shouldn't be gone too long," Junior had told his wife.

"We'll be fine, and the Jensen's are nearby. Mabel said she or Albert would come by."

With the goodbyes said, Edwin and Junior started for the train station.

"I know Pa said he wanted to be buried next to Ma, but that was afore we came out here. I'd like to think he'd like me sending him back," Junior told Edwin as he maneuvered the wagon around some cacti and rocks.

"You got someone to take care of the body and bury it or you going to go all the way?"

"Don't know. I hated to leave Nettie, especially with all the trouble, but," Junior fell silent, then continued, "You don't think they'd..."

Edwin could tell Junior was torn. He wanted to honor his father's wish, but the reason for his father's death made him fear for his wife, son, and unborn child. Looking up, Edwin noticed the sky was suddenly filled with a flock of birds. He was envious of their freedom. He knew he was here by choice, but there was something about the freedom to just be. He wondered if Junior ever felt that way, especially now.

"You sometimes feel the weight of responsibility?" Edwin asked.

Junior smiled, then paused as if trying to give his answer the weight Edwin seemed to want. "I suppose, sometimes. Still, I'm so happy to have my family, but yeah, I do feel it sometimes, like now. This does weigh me down."

The two continued in silence, the sound of the wagon's wheels, the clip-clop of the horses, creating a relaxing rhythm. The sun was sliding in and out of the clouds overhead. Occasionally they saw a prairie chicken that would show itself along with the random pronghorn. Edwin found himself liking this young man and envied him his family and youth.

The longer they rode away from town, the more Edwin worried. He hoped everything would be okay with Mary. He was glad Taylor was around just in case. At the same time, he was hoping that Junior might remember some forgotten clue as to why the men he'd been with in the war were suddenly being targeted and killed if that were the case.

Edwin turned to Junior, "I'm guessing your parents were married after your Pa returned?"

"They married just before he left. According to Ma, they were walking in the snow and Pa wanted to make a snowman. He'd said something like, the snowman would have to take his place as her husband while he was away," Junior became pensive. "Ma always said Pa wanted something special to carry him through, though she didn't catch on right away he was asking her to marry him. They had a Christmas wedding and all kinds of fun food. Ma used to smile when she told that story."

"Quite a story," *And it was* Edwin thought. Far different from own his departure. No one even knew until someone had seen him in uniform and told those back home. His parents were both gone and Mary, well he'd not told Mary how he felt about her, he just left. To be honest, he had hinted at enlisting.

"Most of their neighbors brought a bunch of foreign food, well foreign to Pa. Pa didn't necessarily care for it, but Ma, she kinda liked it," Junior said, breaking into Edwin's thoughts. "She even made that special Greek dish for me once, what was it called – saganaki, that was it."

Pulling up to cross the dry creek bed they heard a shot from behind. Turning they saw six men riding their way. Edwin recognized some of them as the group he and Taylor had met on their way to town. Edwin wondered if they would recognize him.

"Now what?" Edwin groused, to hide his concern.

"You know them?" Junior asked.

"I've run into them before," Edwin said quickly as the group rode up.

"Howdy," Edwin grinned. "What can we do for you?"

The same man as before took charge. He stared at Edwin as if trying to place him but not having much success. "There's some folks tried to rob the good citizens around here. We're checking all travelers."

Junior bristled, an angry retort forming. Edwin placed a placating hand on the young man's shoulder. "You're welcome to have a look, but I have to warn you the body's getting pretty ripe."

The man looked at Edwin, trying to decide if he was serious or fooling. There was also that hint of having seen him somewhere before. "Ken, take a peek," he ordered.

Junior almost came off the seat. Instead, he gritted, "If you must, since some 'rock breaking' types like you killed him."

The air grew tense. Edwin realized Junior had said the one thing that could set off a powder keg. That some of these men were criminals was a real possibility, but if those same men took a notion, well, he and Junior, they'd be losers. Edwin was wishing he was carrying a gun now, but if he were, he would be perceived as a threat. This way, he might be able to talk and ease the tension.

"Can't blame him," Edwin nodded toward Junior, "a hard thing to lose a father, let alone having to open the casket. How about I help Ken take his look, just in case some mummy bats come flying out?"

"What the hell you talking about?" Ken asked, his eyes puzzled and a bit scared. "There ain't no such thing as a mummy bat."

Edwin decided it might be best if he could keep the group off balance, so he continued with his story. "Well, there's some would say there's no such thing, but it's real, I can tell you that. When someone's died and left out in the elements like this man was, well the bats they just attach themselves, bury themselves right in. Over time, they die off, but if you open the box... well they just might naturally think it's time to come back to life. Why I've known some who could live in a casket for years."

While Edwin was talking, he could see most were skeptical, but a couple of the others looked to be turning green. Maybe he could get them scared enough, and some folks were mighty scared of bats, perhaps they'd leave without disturbing the dead. He liked Junior and didn't want things to get any worse.

"Okay," the man grinned at the story, then became serious. "While I admit some of the boys may have crossed the law, they're okay now. But bats? Where'd you get such a story?"

Edwin kept his face as blank as he could. "It's a tale that made the rounds in the war.

Seems some of the bodies made noises and started moving. Then at night things started flying around and ... and as you know, most stories do have an element of truth."

"You do have a way about you. Don't know whether I believe you or not, but any man who could tell such a tale deserves a break," the man said as he turned his horse, indicating the others were to follow. "But you won't always get away with it."

"How?" Junior began.

"Later," Edwin cut in." Now let's get moving in case they change their minds."

With a snap of the reins, the wagon crossed the creek bed. Both men were silent as each dealt with the incident in their own way. Junior, angry, and worried about why the men were stopping and searching travelers. Edwin worrying about Mary and Taylor and what might happen the next time he met these men.

As they were coming close to the railhead, Junior turned to Edwin, "You know, Pa said the war was both the making and downfall of him. When I asked what he meant, he just said he'd learned true responsibility, but that something happened that he wished he'd never seen."

Edwin's ears perked up. Was all this tied to that night he was on guard duty? Evidence was pointing more and more to that conclusion.

CHAPTER 13

Back in town two days later, Edwin was outside Mary's place. He raised his hand and knocked on her door. He wasn't sure of his reception after the last time they'd seen one another. He hoped being away had allowed tempers to cool. He knew that his had. In his hand was a bottle of brandy he'd purchased in La Junta. He wasn't sure about the brandy but thought a glass might help to smooth the waters, calm things down, a sort of peace offering.

He hoped she was willing to see and talk with him, but he wasn't sure. With everything that had been going on, Edwin had become insistent that Mary leave Booming and come back to Kiowa Wells with him. Of course, she'd insisted she would not. She didn't want to leave or remarry. The two had words. Edwin made sure Mary made it home safe. Edwin was very frustrated, and Mary seemed even more so. After a night of reflection, Edwin realized he was frightened, not just for Mary, but for himself. He couldn't understand the connection between Chet, the dead man, and himself. That there was a connection he felt sure. He was still concerned for Mary, but his fear had clouded their conversation. Now, after two days for them both to cool off, he hoped to apologize and start over.

"Hello Mary," Edwin burst out as the door opened. "I've come bearing gifts," he finished with a self-conscious smile.

Mary remained silent, surveying the bottle Edwin held before him. The silence stretched, the evening sounds filling in where the conversation wasn't.

"It's by way of an apology," Edwin said, pushing the gift farther toward Mary. "I couldn't find any flowers."

Mary slowly reached a hand to take the bottle, then turned and went back inside, leaving the door open.

Edwin's heart started beating again. Mary's anger seemed to be thawing. "I thought we could have a drink and a toast to friendship," Edwin stated. Seeing Mary walk away, he added, "Just friends, nothing more."

Mary turned back and studied Edwin's eyes. She relaxed and lifting the bottle said, "Sounds good, but only one glass."

"One glass," Edwin agreed as he closed the door and moved toward the table. When they'd been in her kitchen yesterday, Edwin had been focused on Mary. Now, he looked about, seeing lace curtains on the window along with shelves stacked neatly with dishes. It was clean and organized, but with a feeling of home. It seemed Mary had done some decorating while he was away.

Pouring a small amount into the two glasses Mary brought them over, handing one to Edwin. Lifting his glass and smiling a self-conscious smile, Edwin said, "To friendship."

"To friendship," Mary echoed. "I want you to know, I value our friendship, and at the risk of starting the argument again," Mary paused to sip her drink. "I like the life I've created here. I don't want to leave. I know you care about what happens to me, and I love you for that, but..."

Edwin took a sip, and then answered, "Mary, I just want you to be happy and safe. I plan to stay and help you and Taylor, then I'll return home."

Providing I don't get myself killed, he finished in his head.

Edwin rose and taking the two glasses to the counter, he was almost knocked over as a roaring giant of a man came bursting through Mary's door. At least Edwin thought it was a man. He was covered in skins, his long hair flying back as he lumbered toward Mary.

Regaining his balance, Edwin rushed forward to tackle the man about the knees. He didn't know who this person was, but he would not let anyone hurt Mary. The crash as the two fell to the floor knocked the breath from Edwin's lungs. He heard the creature roar out Mary's name. "Mary!"

The creature rolled over, looking at Edwin holding onto its legs. Edwin saw, as the roar ceased, that the creature was a man. This man turned red-rimmed eyes toward him and roared out, "What in tarnation did you do that for?"

The man slowly sat up, rubbing a knot on his head. and glared at Edwin.

All Edwin could do was stare, no words came. The man reached over and slapping Edwin on the back, demanded, "Well, why? Answer me."

Pushing himself up, Edwin was angry and scared at the same time. He wanted to scoot away, but felt if he did the big man might attack, like the wild animal he resembled. He'd worked with such men before in his store, but none quite as loud and demanding as this one. Finally, Edwin thought of Mary, and he answered, "You come bursting in here, a lady's home, roaring like some wild animal, what was I to think?" Edwin responded. "With all the trouble here in town, how was I to know if you were trying to harm her or not?" His anger grew and overrode his fear of the man as he stood ready to tackle him again if he so much as moved toward Mary.

"Mary-girl," the man roared, despite Mary's presence nearby, "who's this Galahad, and what is he rattlin' on about?"

Edwin saw the glint of humor in Mary's eyes, along with a hint of fondness, but for who he couldn't say. The way she was looking at the bear of a man caused him to feel twinges of jealousy.

"Bear Claw, this is Edwin, Edwin this is Bear Claw." Mary smiled as she made the introductions.

Before Edwin had the chance to answer the big man roared, "Howdy Edwin," clapping Edwin on the back. It seemed this man's normal speaking voice was a roar, and he got over anger rather quickly.

"Bear Claw," Edwin acknowledged, offering the big man his hand. He wanted to sit down but was still not sure of what the man might do next, despite Mary's acceptance of him. He wanted to be ready should he need to come to her aid again. But if the handshake were any indication, he might have some trouble taking the man down if he were prepared.

"So, what brought you to town?" Mary asked Bear Claw, her eyes looking to Edwin as he extricated his hand from the large paw that was Bear Claw's.

"Mary-girl, you ain't gonna believe it!" Bear Claw shouted his excitement a living thing.

"Believe what?" Mary asked, moving toward the table in the kitchen. With a look of apology toward Edwin, Mary put the brandy in the cupboard as if to say, this is ours, special just for us.

Her actions warmed Edwin's heart. Perhaps they really could start over and return to the friendship they'd had as children. It wasn't ideal, but Edwin knew he'd take it.

Bear Claw glanced at Edwin asking in a soft roar, "Can we talk in front of Edwin here?"

"Yes," Mary answered. "Why don't we all sit down?"

As the three moved toward Mary's table, Edwin thought that if it were any other man, he would probably take offense. Now, as they seated themselves, he was revising his opinion of the man. He was a big man and Edwin was surprised he'd not been hurt when he tackled him.

Laughing, Mary answered Bear Claw's question, "Edwin's a dear friend, I think it would be fine."

"If you'd rather I leave," Edwin offered as he started to rise.

"No, please stay," Mary stated, smiling at both men.

Acceding to Mary's wish, Edwin sat back down with the other two at the table. He was glad she'd wanted him to stay.

"Well, Mary-girl," the big man said, "your investment is about to pay off."

With her startled look around, Mary placed a hand over Bear Claw's. "Lower your voice, please. While I trust Edwin, the walls and windows have ears," she admonished in a whisper.

Looking around to see what Mary was talking about, he responded in the same whispered tone, "What's this?"

Edwin leaned in, his voice barely above a whisper, "The town's been," stopping when he heard a board creak outside. Then in a louder voice, he said, "Yes, I've noticed Mary's investment here is paying off. The store is doing very well."

Catching on quicker than he'd expected, Edwin saw Bear Claw nod and add, "That's what I was talking about, the goods she ordered..."

"Oh, Bear Claw, thank you for checking on that when you were in La Junta," Mary said. "That was so thoughtful of you. I was wondering if the canned pears were going to come in."

With hand signals, Edwin indicated he would go around front and out the door there, while Bear Claw would exit the rear door. Mary nodded and continued, "Will you be going that way, or shall I just wait for delivery?"

"I'll head that way now if you need them," said Bear Claw as he headed to the door.

They could hear the whisper of cloth against cloth moving away. Bear Claw burst out the door as Edwin did the same out front. Unfortunately, the listener was faster than either of them expected. Despite their giving chase, the culprit got away. Both returned to Mary's to try to figure out who and why someone would be eavesdropping but failed. Finally, Edwin asked, "What's this about a discovery?"

"Mary here has been grubstaking me and I've found a large deposit of coal. Figure she should know her investment in me paid off."

"Congratulations to you both. If the wrong people hear about this..."

"Bear Claw is careful, and I don't think..."

"Mary, and Bear Claw, with all the strange things happening around here, I don't think anyone is truly safe," Edwin said.

CHAPTER 14

The day after Bear Claw's arrival, the sun rose to a cool and pleasant day. Edwin and Taylor spent the morning walking around town getting to know the people who lived in Booming. Most were pleasant but somewhat hesitant to talk about what was going on.

At noon, the two men headed over to Mary's place for lunch. She closed the store for an hour as the three of them and Bear Claw had a meal of sandwiches and lemonade.

"Thought lemons were pretty pricey," Bear Claw commented.

"These were going bad, and I don't mind. I haven't had such a fun meal with good friends, both old and new, in a long time," Mary answered as she smiled at the three men. It had been fun fixing a meal for someone other than herself.

"Well, I'd best get back to work, the store won't run itself," Mary told the others as she rose. The three men rose with her.

"I'll clean up," Edwin offered. "What are your plans for this afternoon, Taylor?"

"How's about this young whipper-snapper and I take a gander along the outside of town? You know, see what is outside this big city," Bear Claw offered.

"Sounds good to me," Taylor laughed. "You be okay spending time with Mary?" Taylor grinned at Edwin.

"Go on," Edwin said, shooing the two men out. "I'll be just fine," he winked.

Edwin had just finished cleaning up when he heard the door open and Mary's gasp. It sounded like a storm had descended. He rushed out front in time to hear, "Well, ain't you the adventurous one? Don't you dare'n to try to stop us or reach for that shotgun you got under your counter."

Edwin watched in horror as the speaker stalked up to Mary, spit dripping from his yellow-toothed mouth, while the other man moved to the pickle jar, putting his filthy hand inside and pulling out a handful of the sour food. "We've been through this before," he threatened, hand moving to strike Mary as she tried to grab the jar of eggs.

Before he'd time to think it through, Edwin rushed forward and grabbed the offending hand. He was thrown backward as the man's hand swung forward hitting Edwin on the chest, causing Edwin to lose his balance and crash into the counter. As he turned back, he found himself staring down the barrel of a navy colt. Fascinated, he watched as the hammer was pulled back, and the finger tightened on the trigger. The whole scene played out in slow motion in Edwin's mind. He knew his time was limited, but he had to try, as he prepared to roll away.

At the edge of his hearing, he heard Mary scream as the man laughed. Suddenly, the boom of the shot came, followed almost instantly by a second shot. Edwin was moving as quickly as he could, knowing he would feel the blow of the bullet somewhere on his person. Instead, he heard a high-pitched angry scream of pain.

At first, he thought it was his scream, but he'd felt nothing. Glancing at his attacker, he saw the man holding a bloody hand as Mary continued moving toward him. He followed Mary's eyes as she looked toward the door. There, he saw Taylor holding his peacemaker, covering the scene.

The shots and screams were drawing a crowd. "You've got an audience," Edwin said, as the crowd grew in front of the store. "And it looks like these men have some friends coming."

Without moving his gun, Taylor shifted his eyes, first right then left. Stepping from in front of the door to the right, he placed his back against the wall as he continued to cover the scene. Soon the would-be attacker's friends stormed through the door, weapons ready.

"Let's not be hasty," Edwin said, hoping to defuse the explosive situation, hands down to his side. So far, the men had not seen Taylor and Edwin hoped to keep that advantage as long as possible.

Mary walked over to her former attacker. "You piece of—" she started as she looked down at the bloody hand, the bullet groove, a straight deep line across the top. "I wish he'd blown your head off."

"Mary," Edwin softly said, taken aback at the anger in her voice.

"No, these..." she paused for breath, struggling against the fury. "I don't care," she finally said, "they come in here, take what they want, which is bad enough, but I will not tolerate myself or anyone, especially friends, being manhandled."

Just as Mary was finishing her rant, Thornton walked in, surveying the situation. With a nod, the men walked out. Taylor relaxed some as the men left, but did not return his gun to its holster. The situation could still turn sour.

Thornton walked over to the cause of all the trouble, his voice soft he asked, "Did you start..."

"Honest Mr. Thornton, I was just..." the man babbled, fear written on his face.

"He was about to strike Mary, so I tried to stop him," Edwin interrupted.

"Is that true?" Thornton asked.

"You know me," the man said, trying to stand tall, but failing.

"Yes, I do, and I gave an order no woman—especially this one—was to be harmed. You didn't listen." He said as he pulled out a set of brass knuckles. "I cannot tolerate those who don't follow orders."

A look of horror traversed across the watchers' faces and you could see their shudders as Thornton began beating the man about the face and body. So quick was the beating that no one had the chance to stop it before the man slumped to the ground, concern about his hand forgotten.

"I will not tolerate any disobedience," Thornton told the onlookers. "And you, my dear lady, I'm sorry you were accosted, but please don't continue antagonizing the men." As Thornton gave a final look to all, he moved toward the door. Glancing back at Edwin he remarked, "You took a chance, be more careful next time. We will have words later, you and I."

Upon exiting, he nodded to Taylor.

CHAPTER 15

That night, after Thornton's brutal beating of one of his men, the store was unusually quiet. No one even ventured out. The saloons were almost dead. The town seemed to be holding its breath. Mary, with Edwin's help, cleaned as much of the blood from the floor as possible. Neither spoke as they went about the task. Each one involved in their thoughts, so much so that they both jumped when they heard the door slam.

"What the...?" Edwin snarled.

Mary dropped the rag she'd been using as she jumped up, losing her balance in the process. Edwin caught her around the waist from behind, bracing himself backward to keep from falling with her. Briefly, her hands rested on Edwin's before she pulled them away.

"Mary," Edwin began.

"No Edwin, please, not now," Mary interrupted, as she moved forward to see what had startled them.

While they had been working the moon had risen, the stars twinkling as if winking at the world and all its drama. They knew nothing was permanent, that all things grew and changed, that everything was a cycle. The sun rose and set, the moon came out, but the stars shone all the time.

What they saw brought a smile to their faces and relief to their minds. Looking at Mary, Edwin's heart raced at her smile of relief. The door hadn't latched and a gust of wind had blown it open.

"There, see, it was nothing," Edwin said in an *I told you so* tone of voice.

"Thank you, but you're wrong."

"How?" Edwin asked, moving closer, wrapping Mary in his arms, holding her close.

"As long as Thornton has a hold on this town," Mary answered into Edwin's chest, then turned to face outwards, still held in the strength of his arms.

"We will prevail, I promise," Edwin whispered into Mary's ear, chin resting on the top of her head.

Edwin still remembered the day he decided to settle down. Traveling through yet another town, seeing the folks moving in and out of the Mercantile, it struck him this was his gold mine.

He hadn't understood until that moment that he'd been moving past the thing he was meant for.

Finding a likely new town close to the railroad, he set up shop after purchasing it from the former owner. The store was an immediate success. Soon others were coming in from the ranches and homes farther out of town. It had felt good to settle, to help people, and to help build a town, but he would give it all up to save Mary. The problem was, she wouldn't let him.

"You started something good, something permanent," she'd said when he'd offered to sell his business to help her.

Turning away from his reflections of the past, Edwin saw the Widow Murphy's pig waddle past and head to the alley. He let go of Mary and followed the pig. There he found her rummaging through the garbage that littered the alley behind Mary's store.

"Mary," he called, "you need to see this."

Moving from the walkway in front of the store, Mary walked back to where Edwin was standing. She saw him pointing.

"It's just Myrtle," Mary said, turning to go back to the store.

"I know," Edwin replied, placing a detaining hand on her arm. "But watch, see how she moves."

Mary turned back, more to please Edwin than from any real interest. That soon changed as a skunk had entered Myrtle's domain. Like the pirates that roamed the seas, Myrtle's tail popped up, like a flag of challenge, her squeals piercing the air as she charged. The skunk took one look at the charging pig, her curly tail flying high, and turned his back to the charging pig. Myrtle, unaccustomed to dealing with these creatures, barreled forward, pulling up short as the intruder let fly with its counterattack.

The sound of Mary's laughter as they watched Myrtle and the skunk do battle was music to Edwin's ears. As he stood next to her, Edwin felt twenty feet tall, able to do anything. From that rarefied perspective, he realized he was meant to take care of her. He also realized that had they married when they were young this moment and life would not have been as sweet. It was the 'water under the bridge,' the life experiences, that made this time far more precious. She was her own person, honed by the fires of adversity, of necessity. That she still had love to give was a gift beyond measure.

"Oh Edwin," she laughed, her hand resting lightly on his arm, while the skunk, having fired its broadside, was now making a hasty retreat, with Myrtle charging after. "I pity Mrs. Murphy when Myrtle returns home."

"You have to admit, it was an entertaining engagement," Edwin answered, as he rubbed his thumb across the base of the hand on his arm.

Mary smiled, remaining still as they watched the world from the back of the store. A comfortable silence, the two lost in their thoughts, yet accepting of each other.

If my life ended right now, Edwin thought, *I could not die happier.*

The comfortable silence ended as Mary pulled away, "I'd better close up. Thank you for everything." Then she lifted up, placing a kiss on Edwin's cheek.

Edwin remained standing where he was as Mary returned to the front of the store. He heard her moving about, then saw the light in the store go out. Soon it was followed by the light in her living quarters. "I love you, Mary Gilpin, even if you never return that love, I always will." His hand reached into his left pocket, rubbing again the locket he'd carried all these years. "Someday, you will be able to accept this, and know how much you mean to me."

CHAPTER 16

Edwin's clenched fist slammed against the counter. "You don't ever tell anybody anything," he snarled at Mary. Edwin had been questioning Mary about Bear Claw, who he was, and why she'd been helping him. Mary had remained stubborn about their relationship. Edwin had to admit to himself, he was jealous.

Taking a step back, Mary, eyes wide, started to turn away. Pausing, she whirled around, finger raised toward Edwin.

"Isn't that calling the kettle black? Why should I have to tell you anything about Bear Claw? He's a friend, a good friend. And on that same note, why was it so important you had to travel all that way with Junior to take his father's body to the train station?"

Watching, Edwin smiled. He'd been afraid she would run out again, or worse, not talk. Instead, it appeared the years had added confidence.

"What are you smiling about?" Mary demanded her cheeks turning pink, but she held her ground and her temper in check.

"You've changed," Edwin said, eyes twinkling as he watched the emotions flying across her face. "I have to say, I like it. You're right, you don't have to tell me about Bear Claw, but I'm curious. Is he a former suitor, or something more?"

Mary's jaw dropped, only to snap shut, her eyes puzzled. "What does that mean, I've changed? And you didn't answer my ..."

Before Edwin could respond, shouts of anger and menace sounded outside Mary's store. Mary blanched white. The eyes she turned back to Edwin were filled with tearful fear. Edwin snapped around, moving to the front window, eyes scanning outside. The crowd was milling around something in their center. It was from there the sounds Mary reacted to originated. In the half-light caused by the cloud of dust being created by the milling people, Edwin noticed a storm off to the west, its lightning show rivaling the events in its ferocity. It seemed that someone was getting the worst of a fight if that's what it was.

"Move away, please come back," Mary called as Edwin started through the door.

"What's going on? What has you so fearful?" Edwin asked, pausing, one foot in and one out the door.

Mary moved forward, grabbing his arm, "Please," she pleaded, and she pulled him back inside.

Responding to Mary's pull, Edwin followed her back inside. Mary slammed the door and using their momentum, walked to the back of the store, pulling Edwin with her.

At the counter, Edwin stopped, turning Mary to face him. "I won't take another step until you tell me what's going on."

Edwin couldn't reconcile the Mary who had found the courage to challenge him with the woman that now stood before him. Whatever it was, it was more than he'd thought when he headed here from Kiowa Wells.

As the storm moved overhead, the crowd dispersed with the continued lightning and ponderous thunder. With each flash, each boom, Mary's face alternated between fear and consternation. Edwin did not remember Mary being afraid of storms, but it had been many years since he'd seen her. Things could change, they had for him.

Just when Edwin thought his questions would remain unanswered, Mary spoke. "Edwin, I wish I could leave my problems in your capable hands, but I don't want you to get caught up or possibly hurt because of them." Her eyes were asking for understanding but she realized she was most likely just talking to a stone wall. Ed win... well Edwin was just Edwin, but she had to try. "This is something that concerns me and my place in this town," she finished.

"Mary," Edwin started.

"Let it go, Edwin, let it go."

Grabbing Mary's hands, stopping their wringing, Edwin pulled her close, thumb caressing the top of her hand.

The two stood there, no closer to an agreement than they were all those hours ago. Edwin continued to caress the top of Mary's hand, not saying anything. All the arguments, all the questions he'd asked had been met by a resolve he'd been unable to break.

A dog barked, breaking the spell. Mary pulled her hands away, watching as Edwin offered his sad smile. "I wonder," he said.

"Wonder what?"

"What happened to us, our friendship, ou r..." Edwin began, stopping as Mary's fingers stopped his words with a touch to his lips.

"Very well," Edwin conceded, knowing he would do all he could to ease the worry Mary carried, despite her words to the contrary. She was his friend, although he wanted more, he would take what he could get.

The dog was silenced as the sound of galloping hooves carried through the quiet left by the departing crowd and oncoming storm.

Mary stiffened at the sound, turning from Edwin to stare out the store's window. The gray sky was cut with the silhouettes of five men riding into town. Seeing the store, they turned and tying up, walked in.

"Do you have any law here?" The grizzled, wiry man demanded.

"The last marshal was killed," Mary answered, "is there something—"

"Ain't that just—" came from the back of the crowd of men.

"Let the lady finish," the first man ordered, "mind your manners."

"Yes sir," came a contrite answer. "Pardon me, ma'am."

"Sometimes these younger men is like a reindeer in a herd of buffalo," the old man said, then continuing his first question, "Is there someone who could...?"

Edwin could see the worry on Mary's face. He knew her fear stemmed from what happened before he and Taylor had arrived. It seemed the law around this town, and perhaps the area didn't live long. Still, he'd come here to help out and this was one way he could.

"I am sort of an unofficial deputy," Edwin responded to the man. "However, I don't have any real authority, just a citizen's..." He left the rest unsaid as he glanced at Mary. Her eyes widened as she stared at Edwin.

The old man caught on quickly, and with a smile, gently asked, "You scared for him, ma'am?"

"I am," Mary said, "but didn't realize he was serious about..." Edwin could see his words bothered Mary. For his part, he was pleased she cared but wondered how Taylor would take his making himself a deputy.

"Ma'am, the boys and me don't want to see your friend hurt. Still, we got to report the dead man, one of our men, we found on our range."

Edwin noticed the man gave each of the others a stern look as he finished up.

"Yes sir," they said almost as one. Then the youngest blurted out, "We learned there was some uncivilized folks around here, and from the looks of the man struggling across the street, don't think they was wrong. He looked mighty busted up."

"Yes, there are," answered Mary. "The leader, a man called Thornton, likes to go around wearing a salmon silk kerchief and is quite educated and proper. Still, that doesn't make him..." Mary stopped as tears tried to escape, despite her desire they not, as she remembered Stu and the rest of Thornton's men who ran roughshod over all the other townsfolk. She couldn't understand, but then...

Edwin moved closer and with an arm around her shoulders, drew her to him.

"I can take your report and..." Edwin stopped, looking at Mary, then started again. "If you'll give me a minute to finish up here." Edwin offered.

"Guess it's better than nothing," the man said. "Well, we'll head over for something to eat and talk to you there."

"Where will you be?"

"Thought we'd just head over to the saloon."

"Might want to try somewhere less busy. The Cosey Cafe is usually open, may not be fancy, but it'll fill you up for not too much. Plus, they're not so busy we'd be overheard by the wrong people," Edwin added.

"Obliged," the man said as he and the others trooped out. Nodding to Mary and Edwin, he added just before exiting, "Name's Jackson of the 2BarC, just took over as foreman/manager for the owners."

Edwin nodded back, "Edwin, and this is Mary, who owns this place," Edwin turned back to Mary saying, "Mary..."

"I know, this whole mess is just getting bigger and bigger, but why you? Why did you say, oh how I wish..." Mary started then stopped.

Edwin stood, waiting to see if Mary would finish. It was so like her to keep everything inside. He remembered when they were young, she kept things inside, as if to say anything would make her vulnerable. Still, he wished she'd trust him to not use it against her.

"Listen, I need to head over, but I'll be right back," Edwin finally said when Mary failed to finish her sentence.

"By the way, did you ever tell anyone about our escapade in the apple orchard?" Edwin asked, hoping to divert Mary's thoughts as he left the store. It was a secret the two had shared, a thing that had helped to solidify their friendship in the early years.

"No," Mary answered. She watched Edwin head out the door. Why hadn't she suggested he take Bear Claw with him? But then that would put the two of them in harm's way. The more Mary tried to confront her fear, the more fearful she became. To help keep her mind busy, Mary started setting the store back in shape. Last night's business not only emptied her stock but as people were wont to do, they left the place in shambles. Shaking her shoulders, Mary sighed deeply saying, "I decided I wanted to own a store, but ..."

"It's a lot of work," Edwin said, finishing Mary's statement as he walked back through the door. "I've been at it for a few years, and there's never a dull moment."

"But have you ever had a run like last night?"

"No, but then circumstances are quite a bit different here," Edwin sighed, as he righted the washtubs.

"It was a new and pleasant town—then they..." Mary paused, tears starting.

Edwin, catching her mood walked over, and with a short hug said, "The shadows that blanket this land will not last forever."

Wiping her eyes, Mary sent Edwin a sad smile, "But how many will continue suffering in the meanwhile?"

Edwin knew Mary was worried about her customers and the town in general. She hadn't said anything, but he remembered the Mary from his childhood, she always seemed to be caring for strays.

"Oh Mary," Edwin said, patting her shoulder, "We'll see our way through this," then pulling Mary to him, Edwin placed a kiss on her forehead.

"Well, I'll be heading out," Edwin said, moving toward the store's counter. "Forgot my hat," he finished as he grabbed the hat from the counter and headed to the door.

Mary stood in the center of the store, looking around, checking this and that with her eyes. Edwin wondered if she had even heard him. He felt her thoughts were running at full speed, and he worried about that.

"Mary," he said, "if you're..."

"I heard you," Mary interrupted, "I'm just wondering what tonight will bring. Edwin, why did you tell those men you were a deputy of sorts? It has just put you in harm's way."

"Mary, you don't need to fear for me or the dark closing in on this town, I'll be close by and I'll be okay."

Mary turned, her eyes searching Edwin's, "Couldn't you stay here?" she asked in a whisper.

"Mary, this is something I need to do."

"Edwin, I don't ask lightly, I am afraid for you, for the dark that has such a hold on this town. There just seems to be so much evil."

"Mary, it's not the dark, it's the people," Edwin smiled to take some of the stings from his words. "Besides you stepped up, can I do no less?"

"Edwin," Mary said, "we are not back in Iowa, and quite frankly, I'm afraid for you."

Edwin wanted to hold Mary close, to tell her the truth about Taylor and how he feared he would fail, fear of not being enough. If he were honest with himself, he would feel better just staying here with her. Still, there was a certain element in town he could call gallows bait. He felt sure most, if not all, would either end up there with the noose around their neck or shot up somewhere and left for the buzzards. Still, he had to try to do what was right. In the last analysis, Mary's safety was the most important thing. "What you said means a great deal to me, although I doubt you need to worry."

CHAPTER 17

Leaving Mary's store, Edwin went to look for Taylor. He knew Taylor wasn't quite ready to reveal his real purpose for being here, but Edwin thought he might like to hear what Jackson and the rest of the 2BarC hands had to say.

Heading toward the saloon side of town, Edwin wondered again at his response to the 2BarC claims. He'd taken up store-keeping as a nice, pleasant way to be with people, yet not have to harm or kill anyone. The war had taken all that excitement out of him.

Thinking of the war, what it had cost him, drew his hand to his pocket to rub his thumb over the locket. Perhaps he could now give it to Mary. If he didn't, he'd wear a hole in it from the constant contact. He'd already worn it down, and there was a shiny spot where his thumb had caressed the keepsake.

At Micah's place, Edwin found Taylor. "Want to sit in on a meeting with the 2BarC?"

At the mention of the ranch, Micah's head shot up. "They're in town?" he asked.

"Just rode in."

"Thanks for letting me know. Things may get a bit lively," Micah told the two. "There's no lost love between them and some of the people in town."

"Why's that?" Taylor asked

Edwin wanted to hear the answer but felt he needed to get to the meeting. He was already later than he'd wanted. But, Mary needed reassurance, and he'd stayed to give it to her.

"See you in a bit?" Edwin asked Taylor.

"Sure, I'll join you in a couple of minutes," Taylor answered. Then turning back to Micah, "So what's it all about?"

As Edwin was leaving, he heard Micah answer, "Since Thornton and his friends arrived, there's been more rustling going on, and fights..."

Edwin made a mental note to ask Taylor what the rest of the story was as he walked the three blocks to the restaurant. He smiled as he realized the ranchlands had ridden their horses the two blocks from Mary's. Either these men did everything from horseback or, Edwin paused, they might need to leave town quickly, should anything happen. That second thought made Edwin uncomfortable. Still, he'd made his bed, he thought as he entered the restaurant and smiled at the five men seated there. Fortunately, the place was empty, and the cook was in the kitchen, so they could talk unhindered.

Edwin had just sat down when Taylor entered. Seeing the younger man, Edwin waved Taylor over and made the introductions. "Taylor, this is Jackson, foreman/manager of the 2BarC. Jackson, this is my friend Taylor. If you don't mind, he'll sit in and listen. He may be able to help figure out what happened."

"Pleased to meet you," Taylor responded, offering his hand to the older man. Jackson shook and then nodded to the other four at the table. "The one to my right here is Harv, next Joe, then Curly and Sam."

Both Edwin and Taylor acknowledged the introductions, taking in the range clothing the men were wearing and the weapon belts around their waists. It made Edwin a bit uncomfortable, but it made sense given the circumstances in the area.

"So what is it makes you think someone from here killed—?" Taylor began.

"Wilson," Joe answered.

Taylor continued, "Wilson. Where was the body found?"

Jackson shot Edwin a look, then indicating Sam as he answered, "Sam here found Wilson at the northeast corner of the ranch, closest to town. He brought Wilson's body back to the ranch house, then he—"

"Sam," Taylor interrupted Jackson as he turned toward that man, "what, if anything, was different about the body and why do you all believe someone..."

Everyone looked startled as Jackson slammed his fist on the table, "Because Sam says tracks led this way," Jackson growled.

"You may not think about it, but sometimes there is a piece that may be overlooked," Taylor calmly answered, his eyes focused on Sam while directing his remarks to Jackson.

"If we are to get to the bottom of this, all avenues need to be examined," Edwin soothed.

Sam shot Curly a look and with a dazzling grin, he drawled, "Well, when I found ol' Wilson, he'd a hole in his back where someone shot him. Then I noticed a peculiar set of tracks," he continued with a smirk.

Edwin noticed Taylor start to tense up as if to go after Sam. He placed a hand on the younger man's arm. Edwin began, "How about we, Taylor and I, go with you out to the area where the body was found? That way we can check the tracks and eliminate—"

Jackson glared, his face flushing with anger. "Are you implying that one of us...? Of all the miserable—"

Taylor stiffened, but Edwin just smiled, a calm smile, and soothed, "Let's not get riled. Wouldn't it be better to cover all leads and aspects of this death? If we eliminate all of you, no one can..."

"By all that," Sam started, but stopped with a look from Curly.

Edwin took notice of the look but continued as if no one had interrupted. "That way, when the culprit is caught, no one can say we weren't thorough."

"You have a point," Jackson reluctantly agreed.

"How about we all go out to where the body was found? You can remain here while Taylor and I get our mounts. We'll join you shortly and then head out?"

"I suggest that to keep things quiet until we check things out, it might be best if everyone were to remain inside," Taylor added.

"Well, me and Sam here kinda was hoping we could get a drink," Curly said.

"I'm sure you would, but..." Taylor began.

"We'll all stay here," Jackson declared, giving each man a look that brooked no argument.

Leaving the restaurant, Edwin stopped Taylor saying, "I think it's about time..."

"I know, but..."

"Sometimes things don't work out the way we'd like," Edwin said, his hand returning to his pocket and the locket contained there. He had chased a chance, a chance to find Mary. Well, he'd succeeded in finding her, but nothing had changed. He supposed he should be sad, but just knowing he was here to help her, to still be friends, made him happy.

"Ed," Taylor said, "Edwin,"

"Yes," Edwin answered, his focus returning to the present.

"I said, how about you head over and get the horses and I'll stop by and let Mary know where we'll be headed? I'll also tell her the truth of my reason for being here."

"Sounds good, and good luck."

Taylor took off, his steps lighter like a weight had been lifted. Edwin envied him his youth, but he also had a fondness for the younger man that made the envy seem petty.

CHAPTER 18

No matter what she did, her mind would not stop worrying about Edwin. Mary had just replaced the pickles when the door opened. She looked up, hoping to see Edwin, instead, it was Agnes and if the look on Agnes's face was any indication she was about to make a pronouncement that Mary was sure would she would not like.

"My, you've been a busy bee," Agnes started. "As you know, I believe women should be married and take care of a home, but I've made allowances," she paused for breath.

Mary, her temper already on a short fuse was getting ready to speak when Agnes continued.

"As I was saying, I've made allowances, but this, letting men stay overly long, and in your living..."

Mary slammed her hand down on the counter startling Agnes to silence. "I do not have to listen to your suppositions, your judgments, especially when you know nothing about it," Mary declared. "And furthermore, a woman has as much right to decide what her life should be without fearing judgment from others."

Agnes stood stunned, that someone would not heed her advice. She stood breathing rapidly, her nostrils flaring as she started to speak when Mary continued.

"Agnes, I know you mean well, but..." Mary started only to have Agnes sniff in that way she had, then turn and walk out.

"Well, damnation," Mary huffed, stifling further comment as the door opened again. It was not Edwin, but Bear Claw. Mary moved quickly toward the big man.

"Mary-girl, what's got you so excited?" Bear Claw asked, opening his arms.

Mary quickly walked into the older man's sheltering arms, crying, "Oh, Bear Claw, I'm so glad to see you."

"I'm right pleased about that, but I feel there's more to it than just being happy to see me," the big man responded, looking down into Mary's eyes. "What's got you so upset?"

"Edwin, Agnes, myself. I'm worried," Mary rambled on, her voice filling with tears to match the ones rolling down her cheeks.

"Tell Ol' Bear Claw about it," the big man said, pulling Mary over to the chairs, and patting the one next to him as he settled his bulk into the other. "What's got you so upset?"

Mary hesitated, then her old pattern set in. This man had been there when she struggled to bring her child into the world. He'd been there, along with his wife Singing Dove, to bring her back from the brink of death as she struggled with the complications of the birth. He'd found a family to care for her son when they thought she'd die. When his wife had been so sick before she died, Mary had been there to help care for her. The two of them had been through so much. Through it all, this big bear of a man had been the rock she'd needed.

"Edwin has gone and said he was some kind of deputy," Mary blurted out. "That blasted man, it's like he's asking for trouble."

"Mary-girl," Bear Claw started, but Mary wasn't listening. Once the flood started, there was no stopping it.

"And now he's trying to bring that young man Taylor into it. He's going to get them both killed, and then Red," Mary paused for breath, while Bear Claw looked on with a grin, although not as big a one as he felt.

"Red got bruised up, and now Taylor has shown an interest, which means he's going to get into trouble whether Edwin helps or not."

Bear Claw, seeing a chance to speak, openly laughed, which shocked Mary.

"Why are you laughing? This is serious. And Agnes is sticking her nose into..." Mary paused, hand on her hip, glaring at the laughing Bear Claw. That same hand left her hip and swatted the big man on the arm.

"Mary-girl, you do beat all," Bear Claw said as he controlled his laughter. "You may say otherwise, but you care."

"Of course, I care," she shot back.

"Well, I think you care more about Edwin than you admit," Bear Claw proclaimed.

"Edwin is a dear old friend," Mary countered.

"If you say so, but..."

"No buts, and it's not what you think," Mary interrupted, "and yes, I feel better, you old faker."

"See, I told you," Bear Claw grinned. "How's about something to drink?"

With an exaggerated 'humph', Mary headed to her living quarters to get them both some tea while Bear Claw watched, a knowing smile on his face as he followed her.

Bear Claw had just sat down at Mary's table when the store door opened.

Mary headed out front but soon returned with Taylor following.

At seeing the young man, Bear Claw asked Mary, "Tell me Mary-girl, when you was young, what'd you think you'd be?"

"What kind of question is that?" Mary said, shaking her head at her friend. "You know what I wanted to be, we talked about it enough."

"No," Bear Claw said, looking from Mary to Taylor, knowing that they needed to know the truth about each other, but he wanted them to figure it out, not have him tell them. "I want to know, 'cause we were just talkin' back then. I mean deep down inside." He hoped by leading the conversation to the past, Mary would figure it out for herself.

"Well, I surely didn't plan on being a store-keeper," Mary replied, "not that it's a bad job."

"And you do a wonderful job," Taylor added to the conversation, his demeanor subdued. He needed to tell Mary the truth but didn't want to disrupt the conversation.

"Thank you," Mary smiled, "I try."

"What..." Bear Claw started again, and if they didn't figure it out, well he'd just have to tell them.

"It's been so long," Mary started then stopped as she realized she couldn't remember or had never had a dream beyond getting married and having children, both of which she had failed.

Bear Claw watched Mary, seeing the sadness and distress in her eyes. He wanted to help but felt anything he said would only make things worse. He was cursing himself for what he'd thought was a brilliant idea.

Both were surprised when Taylor said, "I had a teacher who said, boldness has genius, I think it's part of a larger quote, but I've always thought it a good idea."

"That don't make sense boy," Bear Claw challenged. "How does that fit what you want to be when you grow up?"

Taylor stepped to the table, his hand reaching for the hidden marshal's badge. His hand felt the shape and what it stood for. He'd come over here to let Mary know what was happening and to tell her who he was. "Well, it seems to me, whatever I decided to do, I would do it boldly. That way I'd know right away if it was for me. That's how I knew I was made to be a lawman," Taylor finished by pulling out his badge.

"What?" Mary began.

"Knew it," Bear Claw shouted.

Taylor returned the badge to its hiding place. "I would appreciate you keeping this to yourselves for a bit longer."

"Of course, but why not let the town folk know?" Mary asked, puzzled at Taylor's actions.

"Mary-girl, are you wanting this young man fitted for a pine box?"

Bear Claw's words hit Mary hard. She was upfront in her dealings with others and just assumed her friends were the same way. Then she caught herself, realizing she had a secret just as dangerous, at least to herself. She trusted Bear Claw, he was the only other one who knew.

"Sorry Taylor, I'm sure you have a good reason," Mary said, placing her hands on the table to keep them from trembling. She'd just thought of Edwin and how he and Taylor had come into town together.

"It's okay Mary, but Bear Claw is right, I need to find out more about the powers in control of this town, this area before I feel I can make a difference."

"So what's your plan, son?" Bear Claw questioned. "Even though Edwin ain't here yet..."

"Edwin knows," Taylor interrupted.

Bear Claw grinned, "Dang, seems Edwin keeps secrets better than most, but if there's anything I can..."

"Yes, he can," Mary added as she smiled at the thought of Edwin and his secrets. Mary wasn't surprised, the Edwin she had known as a child could put a secret in a box, hide it away and continue as if nothing happened. Was that what he was doing now, Mary wondered.

"Thank you for the offer Bear Claw, I may take you up on it," Taylor said. "Now, I've got to get back to Edwin and the 2BarC men. We're heading out to check on where they found the dead man."

Taylor turned to walk out, but glancing back, he saw Mary's pale face and wondered about it. "I'll make sure Edwin is careful. I like him, too," Taylor told Mary, then to Bear Claw, "Keep an eye on things, will ya?"

"Sure boy."

"Thanks," Taylor said and hurried out the door and back to where he was to meet Edwin.

Bear Claw watched the young man stride away. His chance to get the two together and tell them the story faded away. But there was still time. Time for Mary and Edwin, and Taylor, if they could all stay alive.

CHAPTER 19

Waving to the seated men inside, Edwin patted each horse as he walked by, studying the tracks of the five that stood outside the restaurant. It wasn't as if he needed to, but he wanted to give Taylor some extra time to tell Mary the truth of his reason for being in town. Edwin had noticed Mary and Red both had a fondness for Taylor. He liked the young man and was glad he'd been able to help. Of course, how much help he would be remained to be seen.

Edwin had been staring at a track for some time when something clicked. He was remembering the stop at the creek. He was telling Taylor the story he'd heard of how no honest man had ever drunk from that particular creek. They had both looked at each other and started laughing. The track was identical to the one he'd seen that day. Edwin shook his head, muttering to himself, "Well I'll be, maybe there's more to that story than I thought."

Looking up, he caught Sam, Curly, and Joe watching him closely. He waved and smiled as he headed over to the livery.

He suddenly felt excited, but also wary. He would need to be careful. He wasn't sure, but somewhere along the line, he hoped the man whose tracks he recognized, would slip up before things blew up in their faces.

"Wonder if it's one of the men here in town with Jackson, or is it someone on the ranch?" Edwin muttered to himself.

It was a bit of a walk to the livery, and Edwin took in the sight of a town trying to find its personality. Many were going about the business of making a living, and the remainder, like Thornton, lived off the toil of others while trying to control and have it all.

It was like thinking of the man brought him out. Edwin saw Thornton heading toward the restaurant. The thought made him uneasy.

He got the horses and was heading back when Taylor joined him. "Found something interesting," Edwin said. "There's a track that looks familiar, so as we walk by, see what you think." He marveled at the calmness in his voice. It was what he felt like during the war; scared, worried, but calm.

"What?" Taylor asked.

"Tracks and they reminded me of our trip into town," Edwin answered. He then added, "I say we need to keep a sharp eye out. It seems one of the men on the 2BarC, or someone who works with them, could be hiding something. I also just saw Thornton heading that direction, and who knows what might happen with him around."

Taylor nodded as he checked the tracks of the five horses. He started to say something but stopped as the five filed out.

From across the street, Edwin saw Thornton, who, upon seeing the group of men. walked across the street hailing Edwin, "Edwin, leaving so soon?"

"Not permanently, just riding out to look over—check on—an unexpected death. Want to get it done before any rain or dust storms destroy what tracks might be there."

Edwin might have been speaking to the wind as far as Thornton was concerned. He was glancing over the collected men standing outside the restaurant. Thornton specifically focused on Jackson. "You the head of this motley band?" he asked with a sneer.

Jackson's face hardened as he looked over at Thornton, seeing a dignified-looking man with a silk shirt, a salmon-colored tie, and a fitted coat. A far cry from his range clothes. "I'm the foreman/manager of the 2BarC. Arrived about three months ago." Then, eyes boring into Thornton, Jackson continued, "Seems there have been some irregularities out there, been happening over the last year or so." To those watching, the dislike each felt for the other was like a living thing. "Well, I'm sure you'll work your way to some kind of answer," Thornton threw at Jackson. "Edwin, I guess I'll see you back here eventually."

Edwin nodded, "You can count on Taylor and me being back. Especially if my suspicions are correct."

Thornton looked over the group again, ignoring Edwin's comment. He sneered, then turned and sauntered away.

"Was that who I think it was?" Jackson queried.

"Yep, that's the man who claims to run the town," Taylor answered. "Suggest we get started.

The sooner we see if any footprints or other signs remain, the sooner..." He left the rest unsaid.

With a nod, Jackson signaled his men to mount up. Casting a last stern, hateful look toward where Thornton had gone, Jackson, himself mounted and headed out of town.

As the group was leaving, Edwin moved over to Taylor. "Did you notice Thornton hesitating to look at a couple of the men when he arrived?"

"Was watching Jackson, he wasn't too pleased to meet our self-appointed first citizen."

"True," Edwin agreed, "there's more here than we think, and I've been feeling that for some time now. I just worry and wonder how Mary..." Edwin left the rest unsaid as they hurried to catch up.

"I'll keep my eyes peeled. Thornton may think he's leaving no footprints, but I've a feeling he's not that good," Taylor said to the retreating back. He thought Edwin hadn't heard but saw him nod. Taylor figured Edwin had caught the gist of what he'd said. Riding past the saloon, Taylor saw Red step out and throw him a discrete smile and wave. Taylor grinned to himself as he hurried to catch up.

CHAPTER 20

Riding toward the 2BarC, Edwin noticed he and Taylor were being surrounded by Jackson and his men. After what he'd found, having Sam and Curly bringing up the rear, where he couldn't see them, made him nervous. This was one time he wished he had a gun. Well, he'd just deal with it as it came, but it would pay to be extra vigilant right now.

Moving closer to Taylor he whispered, "Need to watch those two behind us."

Taylor nodded his head. His mind was on what Thornton was up to. His actions did not ease the young man's mind when they were heading out. He was especially worried about Red.

The group rode on without speaking, the creak of leather saddles, and the jingle of the reins the only sounds that invaded the quiet of the land. Edwin leaned over to Taylor, "I'm going up to talk with Jackson."

Taylor nodded, and slowing down he let the two behind catch up. He made sure he was riding on the left side of those two. That way he could get his gun into play quickly if needed. He took in the area, noticing again how empty and quiet it was compared to Denver, where he'd just come from. He supposed if the situation weren't tricky, he could grow to love these wide-open spaces. He expected Edwin was used to it, but in many ways, it was so different from all he'd experienced.

"You know, I like that old man, but sometimes he gets mighty persnickety," Taylor told Curly and Sam after they'd been riding a bit. They had not liked that he'd moved off to the side when they rode up. In a louder voice for all to hear he continued, "Now, I bet he's claiming we're going too slow."

Upfront with Jackson, Edwin grinned to himself. Taylor was putting the two in the rear on notice, as the two of them had been getting farther and farther behind. Turning to Jackson, he asked, "Much farther?"

"Not too far, we're close to where Sam said he found the tracks, and it's a bit farther to the main ranch house." The two were slowing down, waiting for the others to catch up. "Don't know what's eatin' Sam and Curly," Jackson added. "You'd think they'd be happy to have the 'law' lookin' into what happened."

Edwin nodded in agreement. The actions of those two warranted added observation.

Heading to the ranch, Edwin let his thoughts wander. Better to wait a bit before he tackled the problem of Thornton. He didn't want to start trouble, for it had a way of doing that without his help. He'd remembered the look of concern on Mary's face when he said he'd help Jackson out. It was the same look she'd given him when they were young. He's headed out here to help Mary. Now that he was here, he was taking on things he'd believed he never would have to deal with again. Still, it was good to know he still could, despite his age.

"We're almost to the house," Jackson broke into Edwin's thoughts.

As the group rode up to the ranch, Edwin took in the house and surrounding buildings. To him, the place, sitting in a small, dry canyon, was perfect. A part of him envied Jackson his job, but he was wise enough to know he wasn't cut out for that kind of life. Still, he said, "Nice place."

"Thanks," Jackson replied, dismounting. "The body's over there," he said as he pointed toward a shack off to the side.

Edwin and Jackson, along with Taylor, entered to examine the body, while the men waited outside. What struck Edwin was the trace of powder burns at the wound site. "Looks like he may have known his killer."

"Why do you say that?" Jackson asked.

Waving Jackson and Taylor closer, he held up the light to the body. "See that powder around the wound? Saw that in the war when the combatants were in hand-to-hand. A weapon that close always leaves powder."

"Whoever it was, it's obvious they were not fighting fair," Taylor observed. "Like something Thornton would do."

"Doubt it could have been him," Edwin said, glad Taylor had brought the issue up. "But since you mentioned it yeah, I don't doubt he could have done something like this or had someone do it."

"That the man back in town?" Jackson began.

"Yep, that was him," Taylor answered, brows furrowed in thought.

"If that's true, well," Jackson paused, thinking through what he'd just heard. "The only hands that have been to town in the last month or so were Curly and Sam."

"I'm not saying they had anything to do with it," Taylor quickly added.

"Didn't say they was, but..."

Edwin watched the two, working through the various possibilities. He decided to let them work it out. He turned back to continue his examination of the body.

Those who died violently haunted Edwin. He'd seen so many during the war. He realized death was a part of life, but he wondered about all the mothers who had lost children, especially to violence.

"Do you know, did he have any kin?" Edwin asked.

"He said he had a sister somewhere in Ohio," Jackson answered. "We sent word back."

"How 'bout we head out to where the body was found?" Taylor asked Edwin. "That is if you are done here?"

"Yes, I'm done. That's a good idea, perhaps we'll get lucky," Edwin added. He was thinking about how this whole region seemed to be exploding. This was the second killing since he arrived. He knew the why of the first one, but he had yet to find the reason for this one.

As the three men headed back to where the others waited, Edward queried Jackson about any knowledge or reason for the killing.

"Nothing I can think of, but there has been some missing stock," Jackson answered. "Any of the rest of you know if he'd been having problems with anyone?" He directed at the hands as he walked up.

No one had anything to add. Mounting up, they all headed back out.

Exiting the area, Edwin was struck again by the stark beauty of the ranch. Rocky upthrust, lined with rows of tan, brown, and red caught the sun and reflected a desert-colored rainbow. Soon they were leaving the green of the home ranch and heading out to the dry short grass and stones that composed most of the range.

Jackson must have noted Edwin's look, for he commented, "Doesn't look like much, but it's good rangeland, long as you don't try to put too many cattle on it."

Edwin nodded, "How's it for winter?"

"Need to bring food out, make sure they have breaks to keep them from wandering or getting lost in some of the storms we get out this way."

"Similar to where I live. But I just sell the supplies, never spent much time chasing critters."

Jackson laughed, "I admit not everyone's cut out for this kind of life; but me, well guess you could say I was born to it."

They'd reached the general area of the shooting. "How about we divide up?" Edwin asked

"Sounds like a good idea," Jackson responded.

Edwin hoped he wouldn't cause problems for Taylor by splitting the group up, but it seemed the best thing to do. Taylor was armed, smart, and probably better able to take care of himself if anything should start.

"Taylor," Edwin offered, "why don't you, Harv, and Curly follow the tracks and see what you can learn? The rest of us will head over to where Sam found Wilson's body. That sound good to you, Jackson?"

"Fine by me. You boys do what the man said and we'll meet up here in an hour or so."

Watching as Jackson gave his orders, Edwin noticed a look pass between Curly, Sam, and Joe. It made him wonder what might be the reason. In his mind, he needed to be extra careful and watchful. He caught Taylor's eye, and the young man returned a slight nod.

"What you want us to do, Jackson?" Curly asked as if he hadn't heard Edwin's suggestion or Jackson's orders.

"Just what the man said, you and Harv head out with Taylor there to search and see if the killer left any tracks, and, if so, where they lead. We'll meet up back here in an hour or so."

"Okay," Curly said. "Well, let's get going, we're wasting daylight."

Edwin watched Taylor ride off with the other two.

"So, you some kind the lawman?" Curly asked after a couple of miles.

Taylor paused. He'd already told Mary and Bear Claw, "US Deputy," he told Curly. The man's eyes narrowed, then he smiled.

"Then we're in good hands," Curly said, kicking his horse into a trot.

Taylor and Harv followed suit, but soon the tracks disappeared into a herd of moving cattle.

CHAPTER 21

Mary watched as Edwin and Taylor came riding into town. True, it had been over twenty years, a few pounds gained and lost, but still, watching him brought back sweet memories of a fun and special childhood they had shared.

Those memories continued on to the childhood game she and Edwin would play. He would be her knight who would slay the dragon that was going to harm her. Of course, there would be times when she would come and save him. Now, she realized Edwin was trying to be that knight of her childhood, but the dragons were men. Men whose dragon fire was bullets and those bullets could kill. Either way, people ended up dead. She wondered what she could do to save Edwin from that fate.

When the two had disappeared from view, Mary turned away from the window as the door to the store opened. The dust and heat from outside were followed by the smell of whiskey, a stronger smell than normal.

The smell preceded Red as she sashayed across the floor toward Mary.

"Mary," she slurred, reaching a hand out to stop herself from falling. "I need some castor oil, ipecac, and turpentine."

Mary paused, staring at Red, wondering what had happened. After a moment she proceeded to see if any of the items Red wanted were still in her inventory. Glancing back over her left shoulder, she saw Red in profile. The strong chin, which was jutting out more than usual. Her nose appeared slightly swollen, along with her eyes, as if she'd been crying.

"Yes, I know I'm not the prettiest girl in this godforsaken town," Red said when she noticed Mary's examination.

"I'm not judging, we all do things we may live to regret," Mary answered, remembering her own choice to give up her child. It was a decision that still haunted her, even though she had been too ill to have made a coherent decision. Still, she had agreed to let the child go.

"I know," Red replied, "you have always been fair, but..." Red finally lost the battle to remain upright and slumped to the floor.

Mary stopped, placing some of the things Red had requested on the counter and then moving over to help the girl. The whiskey smell was strong, but she noticed the tears sliding down the paint on Red's face.

"I know I'm no good, I'm ugly," Red whimpered, making a half-hearted attempt to wipe her tears, but only succeeding in smearing the makeup she wore when working. "All I've ever wanted was someone to care about me." With a hiccup, Red reached her right hand to Mary to steady herself as she rose to her feet. "Pay me no mind, I'm just feeling maudlin. It's just all these no goods in town."

"Red," Mary started, only to stop as Edwin walked through the door. As Mary looked into his eyes, the years fell away. Suddenly she was that popular young girl, full of life, trying to decide who would share her favors. The pull of Red's weight on her arm shattered those memories, pulling her back to the harsh reality of her existence. Perhaps Red's dilemma reminded her of her past, the choices she'd made, and where they had taken her.

Edwin reached over and, putting his arms around Red's ribs, he helped the girl to right herself.

"There you go, ma'am." Glancing back at Mary he smiled. "Mary, you're just as kind as always."

Looking at the two, Red steadied herself and moved toward the door. Before Red had taken two steps, Mary pulled her gaze away from Edwin, calling out, "Give me a moment Red, and I'll have your order ready." Turning, she started putting the order together.

"It's okay, you got a friend here, I can come by and get it later."

"Tell you what, Red," Edwin said moving over to Mary, "I'll help Mary, then I'd be honored to walk back with you."

"You don't have to do that," Red began, stopping as Taylor walked through the door.

"Don't have to do what?" Taylor asked.

"Walk back with Red, after we finish her order." Edwin grinned.

Red was blushing and trying to hide the fact that she was unsteady on her feet. She, for the first time in a long time, was embarrassed by her drinking and her unsteadiness.

"I'd be glad to assist the lady back to her place," Taylor grinned. He'd noticed Red's state of intoxication and it worried him. Still, he didn't want to further her discomfort by saying anything. He felt sorry for her, well maybe not sorry, but concerned.

"Here's your order," Mary said into the silence, placing the order in Red's hands.

Taylor offered his arm, and after a moment's hesitation, Red placed her arm in his, and the two people headed out.

When they left, Mary asked, "So what did you find?"

"Unless I miss my guess, it looked like someone from the ranch did the killing."

"But who, and why?"

"That's what we're going to try to find out. The tracks started toward town, then disappeared into a herd of cattle. The thing was, the distance at which the man was shot seems to indicate he knew his attacker."

Mary watched Edwin, the worry and concern showing on his face. How like him to try to help. It was something she always remembered about him, his caring.

"Well, I'd better go see that Taylor doesn't get into trouble," Edwin laughed. "Thanks for being here," Edwin finished, leaning over and placing a kiss on Mary's cheek.

Mary blushed, and when Edwin walked out, she placed her hand over her cheek. Such a caring and sweet man, she thought. He'd never been one to talk about what he'd done for people, never got any praise, but that didn't stop Mary from her fond memories and the hope that he'd be safe.

CHAPTER 22

Edwin parked the buggy. He'd finally been able to convince Mary to take a break. Now, after church services, she'd agreed to go on a picnic with him. The summer sun cast its warming rays as the two made their way to the creek. Edwin hoped that he could help Mary relax, get away from the town, and its problems, at least for a little while. He knew he needed some time to work through what the 2BarC men had said, what he'd found, and how he was going to handle the situation, although Taylor had been there and would do his part. Still, he felt he needed to do something since he'd told them he would.

"Edwin, what a lovely spot," Mary said as she stepped from the buggy. She reached in to pull the picnic basket out, only to have Edwin take it from her. With his other hand, he caught hers and, grinning, pulled her onward toward the creek.

"Wait until..."

"Edwin is that...?"

The two came out onto a clearing. In front was a creek, the clear water tumbling through the rocks. Its music bringing laughter to the eyes of the listeners.

"It's perfect," Mary exclaimed.

Nothing Mary said could have made Edwin any happier at that moment. Looking at her, his blue-gray eyes misted. He wondered if she remembered the time when the two of them had played hooky from school.

The snow had melted late, and the creeks were running high. The two sat on the bank, feet dangling in the icy water, their shoes, and stockings nearby. Now, they were recreating that memory.

To Edwin, the lunch tasted better than usual. Now, as he looked over at Mary, he shook his head. Seeing her this way brought such sweet memories. That was all they were, he thought, memories. He thought of the gray he'd noticed in his hair as he was getting ready this morning. Memories of youth, of young love, dreams of what could be, were just that, memories and dreams. Now the realities of time, the struggles and stresses of living, replaced those kinder, carefree days.

"You're very quiet," Mary observed, cutting short Edwin's maudlin thoughts.

"Just thinking," Edwin replied, shaking himself, putting a smile on his face. "But we're out here to enjoy the day."

"Can you imagine what others will think, what they will say about..."

"Mary," Edwin interrupted, "sometimes, especially now, with everything going on, you just have to get away."

Smiling, Mary grabbed his hand, pulling Edwin closer. "Do you know, when we were kids, I was always tempted to push you in the water?"

Turning his head, Edwin saw Mary's hand move toward his back, the pressure just strong enough to make him teeter on the edge of the bank.

"No you don't," he cried, turning to grab Mary's hands and move them to his chest. In his effort to grab her, he overbalanced, the two of them barely missing a fall into the creek. Rolling backward on the ground, Edwin and Mary gasped at the near miss, then broke into relieved laughter, which began to die away as they looked at each other.

Edwin wanted to kiss Mary, but hesitated, fearing she would realize his true feelings. He wasn't ready, he needed time to get to know her, let her get to know him again.

The matter was taken from him as Mary reached over, drawing Edwin close as she whispered, "Kiss me."

Hesitating but a moment, Edwin leaned close, intent on dropping a light kiss on her lips. Instead, Mary's arms closed around his neck, pulling him close.

His restraint began to fall away, halted by the sound of steps coming their way.

Edwin moved, his body adjusting to shield Mary.

A shot rang out, the bullet hitting close to Edwin's hand. He jerked back, pieces of wood, stone, and dirt falling away, leaving a large splinter protruding from the top.

Quickly, Mary grabbed Edwin's hand, pulling her kerchief out to try to clean around the area as Edwin gritted his teeth against the pain. Two men, one with his pistol still out, stepped into the clearing. Two others entered shortly after.

Edwin was poised to tackle the four, despite his hurting hand, when Mary whispered, "Don't."

Silence, pierced only by the sound of water, which continued, as it always did, flowing over, around, and through.

"What?" Edwin asked, breaking the silence.

"Let's just say we followed you," a fifth man answered, the same man Edwin had met twice before. "Wanted to have a private conversation."

"You didn't need to..."

"Be glad I did," the man interrupted, "or you two might have done something you would've regretted if what I saw was any indication."

"No, we wouldn't," Mary countered the implied suggestion. "You just..." She stopped, her anger at the man and his companions choking the words in her throat.

"You may be right," he answered. His eyes were like ice and just like an ice sculpture, they were lifeless, flat, and uncaring.

"But, let's don't get distracted," he continued. "I told you we'd meet again, and this time I have a proposition."

"We're not interested," Mary said, as she continued cradling Edwin's hand as she gently pulled him toward the creek.

The five watched as Mary took the kerchief, dipping it into the water then she set about cleaning the wound after she'd removed the splinter.

Edwin struggled to remain conscious, the pain traversing from his hand, up through his body, the world tipping and swaying, shading to various shades of gray.

"Stay with us, man," the man said as he closed in on Edwin and Mary. He leaned in and whispered in Edwin's ear, "and tell us where it is and you needn't worry about getting hurt."

"Don't know what you're talking about," Edwin ground out.

"Best you figure it out if you want to keep breathing," the man responded. "There's not too many of you left."

CHAPTER 23

The next day, Edwin was trying to figure out what the men wanted. He had no idea but began to fear it might have something to do with Junior's father's death. He walked into Mary's store, his hand still aching, but healing. He saw Thornton, talking to Mary about someone he'd killed. Edwin stared at the man, listening, then asked, "Wait, what?"

"It's simple," Thornton told the two, "he disobeyed, more than once, I might add so..."

"But," Mary started.

"My dear, we spoke earlier about this. Don't feel sorry for him, he was his father's son."

Mary and Edwin shared a puzzled look. How could that warrant a man's death? Although they could tell that further discussion was not encouraged, Edwin couldn't stop himself from asking, "If you knew that about him, then why did you take him on?"

"People like him have their use, but sometimes the exercise of discipline creates a tricky situation." Thornton bowed and with a wintry grin, said, "This lesson and discussion are over." And signaling to the other two who'd accompanied him, "It's time to get out of here. It disturbs my sensibilities."

Before any more could be said, he turned, bowing again then left, followed by the other two.

"What did he mean—he'd spoke of...?" Edwin asked.

"He'd warned me about challenging his men," Mary answered, staring after the procession.

"But..."

"Just," Mary paused, "let's speak of something else."

Edwin wanted to continue, but when Mary had that look, he knew he'd get no more from her. "What would you like to talk about?" Edwin asked.

"I don't know," Mary said, and taking a broom she began sweeping an already clean floor. "What have you been doing since leaving Lee County, I mean after the war?" she asked.

Edwin wasn't prepared to tell Mary everything but thought maybe a story or two about his riverboat trips might lighten the mood, perhaps even bring a smile or two to her face. "Knocked around mostly. Spent some time on the river."

Edwin watched Mary's eyes take on a faraway look. "On a riverboat?" she asked.

"Yep."

"I've always wanted to take a trip on one. I used to watch..." she stopped, head down, her cheeks pinking.

"Yes, we'd watch them go by, and then we'd talk about what it would be like."

"I remember," Mary said, "and you were able to follow that dream. I think I envy you."

Edwin watched Mary smile. "I was young, back from the war, and didn't know what I wanted. I knocked around quite a bit."

"What was it like?"

Edwin could see the glint of interest and pleasure as it replaced the shock in Mary's eyes. He set about regaling her with the foils and fortunes of a year on the river. Of snags and shallow areas that could catch and wreck a boat. Time flew as Edwin and Mary talked of the early days as they set about cleaning the store. Their discussion continued into the night.

"I wonder what would've happened if you had not," Mary started, stopping at the look on Edwin's face.

"It's done. We can't go back," Edwin began then, shoulder slumping, the silence stretching as the two wandered through the memories of the past. Turning to Mary, Edwin took her hands in his, "This may not be the time," he said as Mary tried to withdraw her hands, but he tightened his grip as he continued, "What truly matters is we have found...," only to be cut short as Mary with an effort, withdrew her hands, turning away,

"Please don't," she whispered.

"But you're not..."

"Edwin, please I'm so happy you are here. I enjoy your company, but--" she stopped, her eyes turning back to Edwin's.

"But, I'm not Harold, I'm not..." Edwin hesitated. "What's important is that we are still friends," he finished. He realized it was hopeless. His hand went into his pocket out of habit his thumb rubbing the precious locket. A locket he would never be able to give to Mary, for she didn't, never had felt for him the way he felt for her.

"I will be here for you as long as is needed," Edwin added.

"Oh, Edwin, I don't deserve you," Mary said, her voice catching, "you are the sweetest, best friend a person could have."

Moving close, Mary pulled Edwin into a hug, kissing him lightly on the cheek.

Embarrassed and hurt, Edwin nonetheless, returned the hug, pulling back before he did something even more stupid.

"It's getting late," Edwin stated, "and you need your rest."

"Thank you for being here, and--"

"My pleasure," Edwin interrupted, "see you tomorrow," as he put a hand on Mary's shoulder. "Do you need help locking up?"

"If you wouldn't mind," Mary said, jumping as the night burst with the sound of gunfire.

Immediately, Edwin pushed Mary to the floor, covering her with his body. Flashes of light, cannons roaring, pierced Edwin's brain. He reached for the rifle that wasn't there. The time came back to the present. Looking down, Mary's face, the face that had gotten him through those nights and days of the war was there. The memory and reality melted together, and Edwin leaned his face down, took her lips in a kiss that expressed all the longing he'd held in check.

Slowly, after the first surprise, Mary allowed herself to be carried into the blanket of love and caring. Gradually the silence permeated the store and the two lying in the semi-darkness.

"I'm--" Edwin started, then getting quickly to his feet, he pulled Mary up. Dropping his hands, he looked at Mary. "I won't apologize for fearing for your safety and trying to protect you, but I apologize for taking advantage of the situation. Now, I probably should go."

It was a long speech, and before Mary could say anything, Edwin was out the door.

Mary stood in the silence left after the round of gunfire. Quite of its own volition, her hand rose to touch the spot where Edwin's hand had rested on her shoulder when he'd held her down. She still felt the weight of him as he rested on top of her while protecting her.

"Edwin?" She questioned. Yet realizing the silence had no answer for her. She'd always known he was a good friend, and she was comfortable with that. Now, although she'd sensed, for Edwin, there might be more. His kiss confirmed that.

"Edwin, please know," she cried, "I can't be what you want," but how to tell him? She cherished him, even loved him, but not as that kiss told her he wanted. She'd been alone, made her way in the world, too long to change. Yet a part of her responded to the need and longing in his kiss.

Before Mary could answer her question, the door silently opened, and a small figure slid in, crouching to the left of the door.

"Who?" Mary called but was cut short by the shushing sound from the intruder.

"This is my store and I will not be dictated to," she stated.

"Please," came a whisper, "they can't find us."

"Come away from that door and tell me who can't find you." Mary waited for a reply or movement, but when none was forthcoming. "Now, or go back to where you..."

There was a rustling by the door. A small figure came toward where Mary was waiting. Mary watched as another small figure moved, making two.

"Please ma'am, sorry I was bossy," Mary heard the taller of the two whisper, "but me and her gotta stay out of sight."

Before Mary could ask why the commotion outside intensified.

"Find those two," echoed through the store, followed by a scurrying and pounding of feet outside.

Mary waited as the steps stopped in front of her place. She held herself quiet, such a simple thing, and the steps moved away.

"All right, now will you tell me what's going on?" She cast her eyes toward where she'd last heard the scurrying. No answer came back to her. She was getting ready to go search for the two when an arm grabbed her.

"Mrs. Gilpin," Taylor's voice reached through the stunned silence, "I didn't mean to startle you, but..."

"What are you doing sneaking around?" Mary's whispered voice cut off the rest of his sentence. "Enough strange things are going on without you adding to the chaos."

"I'm looking for a couple of youngsters, I want to find them before the others do."

Mary heard the rustling and wondered if Taylor also heard it. If he did, he didn't let on.

Perhaps the two thought they'd found a safe place to hide.

"Why do you want to find them?" Mary asked as she lit the lamp, keeping the flame low, creating shadows everywhere. Anyone looking in would just see her moving about the store.

Catching on, Taylor remained where he was, speaking only loud enough for Mary to hear. "Seems their Grandfather was killed. It may have been the man who was beaten in the street the other day, but that's just a guess. Those who probably done it are looking for them. How they got away and the why..."

Mary cut Taylor off with the finger to her lips. Her ears had caught an out-of-place sound. The silence was followed by secretive steps outside the door. Mary continued moving around, preparing for closing. Soon the steps moved away, and Mary went to where she'd last heard the children. "Speak softly, but tell me, and Taylor, what this is all about. We'll do what we can to help."

The older one, after a moment, started talking. "These men stopped PaPa as we were heading toward a friend he knew. He thought if he could get out of town, we'd be okay. PaPa told us to continue on, but we stopped when we found a place to hide." The child stopped talking as tears formed in both their eyes.

Mary and Taylor could sense the terror as the two girls relived the event. Waiting, the older child soon began, "They were asking PaPa where it was. He said he didn't know what they were talking about, but they kept on hitting him."

"Taylor, this may have something to do with Edwin and those men who accosted us the other day."

"I'll go find him, in the meantime do you have somewhere these two can stay? It won't take long."

Mary nodded, and Taylor headed out the back door as quietly as he could, checking to make sure no one was watching.

"How about we head back to my rooms and you can stay there while we find a place for you to stay?" Mary asked, moving the children back to her living quarters and into her bedroom after locking the front door to the store.

"Maybe we could go to the house PaPa was heading to?" The youngest one offered in a small voice.

"Do you know where or who it was?"

Both children nodded, "No, but we can point to who beat PaPa," the older girl added.

Mary jumped when Edwin and Taylor entered the room. Edwin went to the children, "Who was your Grandfather going to see?"

"A Mr. Logan."

All three adults shared a look. "I don't think you can go there," Taylor told the two.

"Where can we be safe?" the older one asked. "Can we find the men who killed PaPa?"

Taylor bent down to the two. "I think you will be safe if you stay here for a time. If Mary doesn't mind. And I promise you, we'll do all we can to catch the men who did this."

With a nod to each other, the two put their hands in Taylor's. As he squeezed the small hands, preparations were made, and Taylor and Edwin left.

The two walked right back in. "Instead, why don't we hide them in plain sight?" Edwin asked.

Mary and Taylor shared a look as if to say, what is he thinking. Edwin, catching the look turned to the children. "Do you think you could pretend to be Taylor's nieces? It would be a game to trick the men who might want to hurt you."

The two nodded, and then Edwin explained. "You see, if we have you pretend to be Taylor's relatives, and the men happen to come into town and see you, it would make them hesitate, especially now that Taylor's the law."

"They could stay here with me, sorta help out. That way someone would always be around," Mary offered.

"We didn't ask your names," Edwin said.

"I'm Lilly," the youngest said, "and this is my sister, Rose."

"Well, Lilly and Rose, we're going to have you go with our friend Bear Claw early tomorrow morning," Edwin began, "then, he will bring you back into town so everyone can see."

"And then we can be with our Uncle Taylor?" Lilly asked.

"Yes, and he will have you stay here with Mary, Mrs. Gilpin," Edwin answered.

The two girls put their heads together, while the adults worked out a plan. Taylor would locate Bear Claw and have him come by. Soon the girls turned to the adults. Rose gravely said, "We'd like to be your nieces. Mother's name was Dolly, she and Daddy are dead. That's why we were with PaPa."

"It's a plan then," Taylor said as he knelt to the two girls. "So Dolly was my sister, but died, and you've come to live with me."

The girls nodded, then came over and hugged Taylor around the neck. Edwin and Mary shared a look. It seemed as if things were going to work out for the girls, at least for now.

"What are we going to do when they are safe?" Mary asked.

"Well, guess we'll cross that bridge when we come to it. Maybe they have actual relatives somewhere," Edwin answered. "In the meantime, we can hopefully keep them safe and find the men who harmed their grandfather."

CHAPTER 24

The next day Mary was busy with the books, and it always put her in a bad mood. She should've seen the writing on the wall, but somehow the excitement of the store and the new town had blinded her. Now, she was in and was having trouble finding a way out. In addition, with the girls here, well, she wasn't willing to give up. She had tried that, and it'd taken almost twenty years to leave it behind. And here was Edwin coming back into her life, willing to bail her out. Not this time. This time she'd make it on her own.

Closing the account book with a bang, Mary looked at her own little corner of the world. "Never again will I depend on another," she told the store walls, "I've made a life here and..."

The door banging open, as Mary was turning away, stopped her thoughts. Whirling, her eyes met a pair of cold ones. Looking at Stu, Mary wished she was back under the pine tree, surrounded by the multicolored wildflowers that gave her such peace. The girls, hearing the noise, had come in to see who it was. At a nod and wave from Mary, they returned to the living quarters.

"So, Mrs. Gilpin, Mary, have you an answer to my proposition," Stu grinned, his eyes colder than ever.

Mary and Edwin had discussed the matter at some length. Taylor had let Mary know about the protection payments the others were making. Mary had told them of Thornton's words. While they weren't sure some of the other men wouldn't try it on her, they'd agreed, should it arise, she'd decline. Now, looking into Stu's eyes, Mary had her doubts.

"I've thought about your offer," as her hands clenched and unclenched beneath the counter. The shotgun was close to hand, but to even move toward it would surely bring dire consequences. She believed Stu was aware of the weapon.

"You know the boss only has so much patience," Stu countered. "You bein' a woman, he's been more patient than with the others."

Mary's mind went back, back to the day she'd run away. She'd been threatened then and looked at what had happened. Mary felt herself being backed into a corner. "Not again," she whispered, as the constrictions in her chest grew tighter. She was done caving into threats.

"I appreciate his kindness, if it is him and not just you," Mary replied forcing a smile. "But this is not something that can be rushed into."

Stu moved closer, his mouth twisted up in what Mary took to be a grin. Pulling the knife from his scabbard, he hit the sack of flour, ripping the blade down the whole length.

A quick intake of breath from Mary drew the man's eyes toward her again. Stu grinned, "Just to get your attention. Twenty-four hours, then—" Stu motioned again to the flour sack, "Twenty-four hours," he cackled, leaving the door standing open behind him.

Sagging against the counter, Mary let the tears she felt film her eyes, but stopped short of letting them fall when the girls came in. Seeing them and noticing the flour hadn't all spilled out, Mary grabbed the scoop and set about salvaging what she could. She might not be able to sell it, but she could use it to make baked goods.

"Can we help?" the youngest, Lilly asked.

"Would you go back and grab some large bowls to put this in?"

The two scampered away as Mary said quietly, "You will not win," the words echoing softly through the empty store.

Edwin and Taylor walked in as Mary and the girls finished cleaning up. Both shared a look after a glance at Mary, the broom in hand, the flour on her cheek, and the girls carrying bowls of flour to the back.

"Don't say a word," Mary warned, as she marched to the back of the living quarters.

"When she's calmed down, perhaps we can get the full story about what happened here," Edwin said, clapping Taylor on the shoulder.

CHAPTER 25

"Mary, you don't have to do this by yourself," Edwin insisted, his hand out, taking hers in his. He and Taylor heard the story of Stu and his threats. Now, Edwin was trying to do what he could to convince Mary to let him help.

"Edwin, we've been through this before," Mary answered, attempting to pull her hands away, only to have Edwin's grip tighten. "I have been taking care of myself all these years."

Edwin gazed at her face and saw the face from his past overlay the current one. He still saw the smooth skin, the sparkle in the eyes. The sparkle was still there, but lines now etched themselves around those eyes. Smiling, and pulling her close, Edwin glanced out the store window, "Mary, don't continue to hang yourself on the hanging tree for something you had no control over."

Mary's eyes grew large; shock, then anger, followed by tears. Finally, Mary jerked away. "How dare you?" Her words echoing as she walked away.

Edwin followed, he struggled with the idea or to find an opportunity to give Mary the locket he bought all those years ago. That he still wished to marry her was a given. That she would turn him down was also likely, at least in his mind. Regardless, he wanted her to have it. The way things were going, he'd probably be dead soon. He believed there was someone, probably the men who'd accosted them at the picnic, who were after something he knew nothing about. The probability of him ending up like the others was growing daily.

Mary had gone outside, probably to keep the girls from seeing her upset. Edwin approached cautiously. "Mary, I'm sorry if I've offended you, I just want to help."

"I know, but it's hard, especially after all the years of taking care of myself." To divert the conversation Mary called, "Edwin, look, I've never seen a butterfly that looks like one."

Edwin shook himself out of his brown study and looked to where Mary pointed. Then moving closer, he put an arm around her waist. "Me either. Think it got lost?"

Mary laughed, "Butterflies don't get lost, do they?" she asked, glancing up.

"You never know," Edwin answered, looking at Mary. He felt like she was offering him a box of candy, but he wasn't ready. Still, he felt his left hand move toward the locket in question. His hand wrapped around it, and he started to bring it out, but fear took over and he let go of it as if it had burned him.

"Edwin, is something wrong? Is your hand still hurting?" Mary asked as she saw his hand jerk.

"No, just remembering."

"I still think about some of the trouble we got into when we were children," Mary stopped, as a fit of giggles took over.

"What are you...?"

"Remember when we put turpentine in the Webster's milk pail?"

Edwin cringed, then began laughing himself. "They couldn't figure out why the milk tasted so off."

By this time Mary was doubled over, "And then we followed that up with linseed oil in the hay."

"It's a wonder we weren't caught."

"It is," Mary said, then she hiccupped. "We had some fun times."

"Yes, but I wonder how we would feel if some child had done that to us?"

"Probably pretty upset. It's a wonder we turned out as well..." Mary stopped.

Edwin waited, knowing she must be remembering.

"I guess it's like turning back the pages of a story and reliving them again. We did have quite a time back then, didn't we? But then we put them in a box and keep them tucked away, both the good and the bad," she added.

Thinking of his trials during the war, he understood what she was saying. It had taken years for the memories and nightmares to fade, only to have something happen to bring them to life again.

"I would say we do," Edwin agreed. It was a lesson he'd not forgotten, but he wondered if he'd learned it too well. Now, he was again thrown into a battle zone despite all his efforts to remain peaceful. Then he thought, the irony was, he put himself here by choice and it was not in him to give up.

The two stood in silence, each lost in their thoughts, holding each other, without realizing they'd moved together.

"Well, I'd better get going, got work to do," Edwin said, breaking the mood and putting space between them.

Mary felt Edwin moving away, leaving a chilled space where he had been. Part of her wanted to pull him back, recapture a piece of what she'd felt, despite her thoughts and words earlier.

The two walked back into Mary's store. Despite it being early, the saloon side of town was as rowdy as ever. They had just passed the threshold to the store when Edwin felt a slap on the back of his head, then he was being pulled backward.

"What the..." Edwin growled as Mary screamed.

Then Edwin was dragged across the street and pushed through a door. There, he was greeted by what he thought was a semi-circle of men standing in the dark, each silent and probably staring. He heard Mary's voice calling his name, but when he turned he was met with another shove.

"If you hurt her, I swear you can't run..." Edwin threatened, only to be cut short with another—harder—shove that had him struggling to keep his balance. He wanted to turn and confront his attackers but was more fearful of those in front of him. The area was too small, and there were too many men, for any kind of combat to be effective. Well, he'd a feeling this time was coming, it just happened sooner than he'd expected.

Glancing backward, noting two men guarding the door, Edwin heard a voice say, "Relax, Mrs. Gilpin will be fine."

Edwin knew it was Thornton by the sound of his voice. Edwin watched as the man slowly came from the dark in front of him. Thornton walked between the men, as they made away for him, then they closed rank again. Despite his efforts, Edwin could not make out the faces of any of the men with Thornton.

"What do you want and why the threats and theatrics?" Edwin asked.

"What we have to discuss is not for delicate women's ears."

Edwin snorted, then remembered what Mary had said about Thornton and his words to her. "Very well, what can I help you with that couldn't be accomplished without just asking to speak with me?" Edwin asked, looking directly into the eyes of the man in front of him.

Someone had lit a lamp, casting light on Edwin and Thornton. Edwin saw Thornton smile at his question. Again, the same smile that did not reach Thornton's eyes.

"It's come to my attention that you may know the whereabouts of a certain set of objects taken during the war when you were in Missouri."

Here it comes again, Edwin thought. Try as he could, there was no memory of anything except that one night on guard duty. "I don't know what you are talking about. I never saw anyone take anything, nor did I."

"Come now, you don't expect me to believe that?"

"Believe what you want, I don't know anything about any stolen anything. Did it happen? Well, I imagine it happened on both sides, it was war."

Without warning, Thornton threw a punch into Edwin's ribs, doubling him over as the air exploded from his lungs. The two who'd been guarding the door moved forward, holding Edwin up. "Now, let's try this again," Thornton grinned.

"Can't tell you what I don't know," Edwin squeaked out as he pulled air back into his lungs, catching as the pain in his ribs grew.

"Oh, you'll tell me, or I will have to break my promise to Mrs. Gilpin," Thornton swore, walking away. "I'll give you two days, that's all. After that, all promises are null and void."

Edwin found himself propelled back through the door and with a shove, he landed on the ground, the door slamming shut behind him. He stayed that way for a few minutes, then struggling to rise, he dusted himself off and went in search of Taylor.

CHAPTER 26

After Edwin told Taylor about his meeting with Thornton, the young man set about finding trying to find out what it was he was after. Mary had reservations, but ultimately agreed and also set about trying to question others discretely. Now, three days later, they were no further along. Edwin was heading out to meet Taylor when he heard something that chilled him.

"A few final words for you marshal, afore we pass judgment," Edwin caught as he started around the corner from Mary's living quarters. It stopped him in his tracks. "What's going on?" Edwin said under his breath. He couldn't let them dispose of yet another lawman, especially Taylor who was like a son to him. The thought startled him, but he realized he'd come to feel like Taylor was the son he would never have.

Well, you've done stupider things, he told himself. He turned, quickly returning to Mary's store. He wasn't sure how much time he had, but he'd be damned if he'd not try. Mary shot him a glance when he grabbed the shotgun, for she knew Edwin's aversion to guns. At Edwin's nod toward the window, she moved over, seeing Taylor and the others surrounding him.

The positions of the men around Taylor were such that the corner he'd recently vacated was the best place to do what he was planning. Now, he needed to get there without the others hearing or seeing him. He hoped that the element of surprise would do the trick.

"Edwin, what are you going to do?" Mary asked as she glanced out the window once more.

"Just taking care of little business, don't worry." Of course, he knew Mary would worry, he just hoped that she would remain indoors until it was all over. Shooting her a smile, Edwin left out the back. He moved as quickly and quietly as he could to the edge of the alley he'd vacated. He was just in time to hear "We here run this town, you and your kind ain't necessary."

"If that were the case—" Taylor began.

"I ain't finished," the leader growled as one of the other men made a move toward Taylor, only to be waved back.

"Now, as I was saying," he continued, "we don't need you here. We're giving you a choice, mount up and ride off now and you live, otherwise, you can stay here permanent like," the man cackled.

Edwin knew Taylor would never back down but was he good enough to back whatever Taylor would do? Could he help? No matter what his choice, would it make any difference to Mary? Edwin's hands shook. He'd sworn never to kill another man, yet here he was ready to do just that. "Enough with the doubts, old man," he whispered. "You can't let Taylor die."

Edwin bumped the barrel of the shotgun against the building's corner. The unexpected sound startled the men, including Taylor, who used the distraction to reposition himself.

"Seems a bit one-sided to me," Edwin called out, "mind if I join the conversation?"

Seeing the odds had changed, the group backpedaled a bit, but did not give up entirely as the leader growled, "This ain't none of your concern."

Taylor glanced at the other two. Now that he was out of the box they'd had him in, the men looked nervously around. His sudden move when Edwin had spoken, had foiled their plans. Keeping a watchful eye on the other men, along with the leader, Taylor was willing to let Edwin call the shots. He had to admit, he was never so glad to hear the old man's voice. Although if he were honest, Edwin wasn't really all that old.

Edwin called out in answer, "It's my concern when it comes to the people in this town."

Looking at the new situation, the leader who'd believed this would be an easy thing, now saw that removing the new marshal would be a bit tricky, if even possible. Perhaps cutting their losses might be the better option. Still, he couldn't allow himself and the men to lose face. "You may be right, but things can change mighty quick, you just remember that," he shot back.

"As they say, the past is smoke," Edwin began.

"And when necessary blow it away," Taylor finished as he pulled his pistol. "Now you can take up residence in the jail, or—" he let the rest hang.

Watching the three, both Taylor and Edwin were prepared for the crash of guns, and the literal smoke they spoke of, filling the area. Taylor could tell the speaker was tempted as his hands started to move down, but the others stared at the shotgun barrel, backing slowly away, hands held high. Seeing his men back up, the leader slowly raised his hands.

Careful to stay out of the shotgun's line of fire, Taylor relieved the three of their weapons. With Edwin's assistance, the town added three new residents to the local lock-up, such as it was.

After taking care of that chore, the two of them headed back to Mary's store where they ran into Bear Claw.

"Come on boys," Bear Claw exclaimed, placing an arm over their shoulders. "You did a mighty fine job out there."

"You saw?" Edwin asked as he returned the shotgun under Mary's counter. He shot her a look of thanks, noticing his hands no longer shook. A part of him was relieved, another worried that he could pick up where he'd left off all those years ago.

Taylor shot a look at Edwin then turned to the old man. "Why didn't you..."

"You had the matter well in hand, didn't want to make it worse," Bear Claw interrupted. Taylor had no time to reply as shots echoed from across the street. Taylor was heading out the door just as Edwin caught a movement and lunged to grab the young man, shouting, "Look out Tay, they're outside."

The last thing Edwin wanted was for Taylor to take up permanent roots in the place. Especially since they had just avoided a comparable situation. It seemed someone was determined to remove Taylor from office and plant him in the area permanently.

When Taylor had arrived to take over the job of marshal, Edwin knew the young man had given himself twenty-seven days to make the town safe again. Now Edwin was worried that Taylor might not even make fifteen days.

Glancing back at the two older men, Taylor nodded his thanks as he removed Edwin's hand from his arm, and turning, he moved to exit the rear of the building.

"We gonna let the kid take this on by his self?" Bear Claw asked, shooting Edwin a look. Edwin looked embarrassed. He could defend himself, he'd just gone through a similar situation and survived, but to go again so soon made his hands start to shake. Still, what Bear Claw said was true, he not only owed it to Mary and the town, he owed it to Taylor.

Not sure what the older man had in mind, Edwin queried, "What can we do? He won't know we're helping, will he?"

Bear Claw smiled, "Oh, I think we can be of some use without getting ourselves shot up."

"How?" Edwin asked, hoping the man had a plan that didn't involve guns or shooting. He wasn't sure he wanted to do that again soon.

"Listen close," Bear Claw beckoned.

Edwin moved closer as Bear Claw laid out his plan to help Taylor without getting themselves shot up in the process. Listening, he wasn't sure it would work but realized it was better than just standing around. With luck, the plan just might work.

Both Edwin and Bear Claw began punching each other as they made their way out the door and down the street.

"Come on, Edwin, make it look real, slug me hard enough so's I fall a few times," Bear Claw demanded.

"What if I..."

"Don't worry about it," Bear Claw answered while throwing a punch at Edwin's head. It had enough power to sting. Without thinking, Edwin drew back and punched the older man in the ribs.

Falling to the ground, Bear Claw shouted, "I may be in the autumn of my life, you don't hit worth—"

Finally catching on, and realizing they were both in better shape than they thought, Edwin replied, "The way you hit, it's more like winter." Edwin threw a punch at Bear Claw's head but failed to connect as the older man weaved away.

"Boy, I was climbing mountains when you was in..." Bear Claw started but was cut short as Edwin threw a monster of a left that caught the older man on the shoulder, throwing him back.

Bear Claw shook himself then launched into a run. A run that caught Edwin in the stomach, pushing him back against the wall of the nearby building.

The two were drawing quite a crowd. It was as if the dam had broken as the stores emptied their customers, and the street filled around the site of the moving battle.

All was going as planned. Both Edwin and Bear Claw could see Taylor moving toward his would-be shooter, who'd been distracted by the fight. Then Mary came storming out of her store, shotgun in hand.

"What do you think you're doing?" Mary demanded as she fired a barrel toward the sky.

The two stopped, taking in the sight of the petite woman with the shotgun, "I won't tattle," Bear Claw winked at Edwin.

Mary glared at the two, and Agnes, the mayor's wife, moved to strike Edwin in the ribs with her umbrella.

"Ouch," Edwin exclaimed.

"Teach you to fight in the streets," Agnes said, every other word punctuated with a poke of her umbrella.

"Now listen," Bear Claw and Edwin both said when they heard a shot, followed closely by another off to the side.

A hush fell over the crowd as the would-be assassin fell from the second-floor window of the hotel.

Looking to where the second shot originated, they saw Taylor pulling the man up after he'd holstered his gun. Cuffing his groggy prisoner, he glanced over at Edwin and Bear Claw, then at Mary.

"After you take care of your bruises, come over to Micah's. We can't have people fighting in the streets," Taylor ordered the two. If they'd looked closely, they would have seen the twinkle in Taylor's eye, but he was too far away for any but his prisoner to see, and he wasn't looking.

CHAPTER 27

The town was quiet for the next three days. Edwin and Taylor headed out to the 2BarC to question some of the other men. Edwin had stayed to talk with Jackson, who was upset about Thornton and the possibility that he may have been involved somehow. Taylor felt Edwin would be better able to handle the older man, so he returned to town. He was caring for his horse when Thornton walked in.

"So, you thought that you would sneak in and then slowly decimate my men?" Thornton asked standing near the door of the barn. "It's not going to work."

"You can call it any way you wish," Taylor replied a smile on his face. He continued, placing the saddle over the stall, "I came into town to get up close and personal with the inhabitants to see who warranted extra attention. That you and your men stood out is your problem, not mine."

"Call it what you will, your services are no longer needed in this town," Thornton declared.

"You have no say..." Taylor began as he moved toward Thornton.

"I have all the say in this matter. We've done nothing wrong here," Thornton stated. He turned away to leave as Taylor's words stopped him.

"I think extortion and possible murder qualifies."

"And you can prove such a ridiculous claim," Thornton declared. "You have witnesses?"

Taylor realized he let his anger at this smug man get the better of him. Cursing himself, Taylor looked Thornton in the eye, "You'll find out."

Thornton glared at Taylor and, finding no effective way to get further information or to threaten the young man, he left.

Taylor released his breath as he relaxed slightly, knowing his life was now considered an open season for Thornton and his men, even more so than it had been the past week. He still wasn't sure he could get anyone in the town to support him, they all seem too frightened. All except Mary, Edwin, and Bear Claw, who'd been acting as his jailer.

Thinking of Bear Claw, he wondered if Bear Claw was at the so-called jail, or around town somewhere.

Taylor followed Thornton out the door. As he exited, he barely escaped being hit by a wasp hive. Despite the hive missing him, the insects managed to strike his hands and face before he escaped back into the barn, slamming the door behind him. While it didn't keep all the wasps out, it cut down on the number stinging him.

"Got him. He'll be out of our hair for a while," Taylor heard from beyond the opening, as he headed for the rear of the barn. The wasps were beginning to disperse and other than some swelling, Taylor felt okay. Walking out the back entrance, he slipped out and around to the front in time to see two men calling after Thornton.

"Mr. Thornton, that reward for getting the marshal," what he intended to say froze on his lips as Thornton turned. Thornton caught sight of Taylor as he walked up to the scruffy man and hit him hard with a backhand to the jaw.

"I have no idea what you are talking about," Thornton snarled. "Now the two of you get out of my sight, or better yet, leave town."

The man struggled up from the ground with the help of his friend, "But I thought—"

"Out!" Thornton snapped. He turned his gaze to Taylor. "You look a bit worse for the wear, better get those stings taken care of." Thornton nodded, then headed for his office, glaring at the men he'd ordered out of town as they rushed to their horses and galloped away.

Taylor watched the whole scene with interest. He was pretty sure Thornton had put a bulls-eye on his back, but how to find a way to prove it? He headed toward Mary's store. She should have something for the stings, and perhaps Edwin was back, or Bear Claw was around. He needed help, now that they were resorting to other methods of getting rid of him, as much as he hated to admit it.

Walking to the business district on the next street, Taylor made it to a point to be aware of his surroundings. That it was proving to be more difficult, Taylor noted, as his reaction to the stings was setting in.

Moving by the Milk Swamp Restaurant, Taylor lost his footing as a wave of nausea overtook him. As he caught himself, and his eyes regained focus, he found himself staring at a door.

"Never noticed that before," he whispered through chattering teeth. Then he turned toward the restaurant entrance, wondering again how a place called the Milk Swamp had any business.

"Need to get to Mary's," Taylor told himself as he turned away and staggered up the street, the doorway's mystery vying for focus with the reaction raging through him. Swaying, Taylor stopped in front of Mary's store. As he reached to open the door, the world turned a wild array of colors before fading to black.

Mary jumped when she heard something crash through her front door. Rushing forward, shotgun in hand she almost fell over the prone figure lying on the floor. The body was lying half in and half out. Laying the gun to hand, she struggled to turn the body over, fear of what she would see. When she realized Taylor was the body, she blanched. Leaning over, she saw he was still breathing, but just barely. She was relieved but wondered at what had caused the marks on his face and hands.

"What happened?" She asked the still figure on the floor.

"He's been stung," Little Bobby answered.

Mary hadn't even heard the child come in. "He what?" she asked.

"They threw a wasp nest at him, and some of them stung him," the boy told Mary. "I was playing by the barn when I saw it."

"Oh no," Mary whispered, leaning closer, feeling Taylor's forehead which was burning hot. "Did anyone see you?" Mary asked Bobby.

"Don't think so, ma'am."

Rushing back to her kitchen, she brought back towels and water. She began bathing Taylor's face and hands. How she wished—she stopped, "Bobby, have you seen Edwin, Mr. Markham, or Bear Claw?"

"Saw Bear Claw earlier," he answered.

"Will you go find him and bring him back? If you see Edwin, tell him, too," Mary requested. As the boy started out the door she added, "And ask your mother if she would mind sharing some of her marigold blooms with me?"

"Yes, ma'am," Bobby answered as he rushed away.

"Please hurry," Mary called, as she continued to treat Taylor right there on the floor of her store. She was hoping and praying he would respond.

"The door, the door," Taylor started chanting.

CHAPTER 28

Mary heated a cauldron of water to wash the sheets Taylor had been lying on. After four days, he was able to get up and move around. Mary smiled, for it had been a challenge to keep him quiet after the first thirty-six hours.

Hearing steps behind her, Mary stiffened, fear closing in on her. She relaxed when she heard Taylor say, "Anything I can do to help?"

"You can help me empty the water when I'm finished if you feel up to it. I still think you're up and around too soon."

Taylor nodded, "I'm doing okay," as he sat on the log watching Mary. He still wasn't sure he believed Bear Claw's story about her being his mother. He had no problem with Mary. She had stayed by his side, taking care of him as he fought his way back from his reaction to the wasp stings. It was after he was coherent that Bear Claw had come in and told the two of them about the relationship. They both had been stunned, but it had been Bear Claw, who'd cared for Mary when Taylor was born and had arranged for Taylor's 'parents' to care for him. He'd kept track of both through the years.

"Why didn't you say something sooner?" Mary had asked.

"Didn't want to make the situation any more stressful than it already was. Now, with Taylor almost dying, well, I figured it was time."

They had accepted his explanation, but there was still some awkwardness between the two.

"Mary," Taylor started, then hesitated, when he thought about what he was about to say.

"What?" Mary asked, forearms moving up and down as she worked to clean the sheets. Pausing she glanced at Taylor, seeing him blush and fidget. With a grin she began, "Are you wondering about what Bear Claw said?"

Taylor nodded, then jumping in. "I don't want you to think—"

Wringing the sheets, Mary placed them in the empty tub, "I don't." She smiled and continued, "Now, how about you empty the tubs while I hang the sheets? Afterward, we can go inside and talk."

Taylor rose and did as Mary asked. The two returned inside, after the sheets were hung, with some help from Taylor. Mary busied herself at the stove. "How would you like some ham? I can caramelize some onions and corn to go with it."

"Sounds good, I do admit I seem to be hungry all the time," Taylor answered. After taking a seat he continued, wincing as he did so. He grinned. "Seems I'm not as recovered as I thought."

"Doesn't surprise me, you were mighty ill. I used almost all of Bobby's mother's marigolds creating a poultice to take down the swelling and draw out the poison."

"I want to thank you for all you've done."

Mary moved over to place a hand on Taylor's arm. "You're welcome."

Taylor gave Mary a crooked grin. "We're avoiding the subject, aren't we?"

Turning away, Mary raised a hand, wiping at her eyes. In admitting Taylor was her son, and she knew he was, she and he both would become even more vulnerable if the word got out. Still, he was—she stopped. Dishing the food onto the plates, Mary took them to the table. Taking a seat, she answered Taylor's question. "Yes, I believe Bear Claw. You are my son."

"Are you ashamed of me, what I..."

"No!" Mary exclaimed, interrupting Taylor. "Let me tell you the story."

Taylor waited, but as Mary remained silent, he bowed his head and began to eat. He was struggling with his feelings. He was afraid of what Mary might say. Afraid she had purposely given him up as unwanted. His thoughts were interrupted as Mary began talking.

Mary placed clasped hands on the table, her voice soft. "As I stood in the graveyard, staring at your father's grave, I knew I had to leave. People in town were already starting to shun me because of what they said he had done. If I hadn't been with child, I might have stayed and fought back. But I didn't want our child—you—to grow up with that stigma."

Taylor stared at Mary as she told her story. He couldn't imagine what she'd been through. He began to understand how things could drive someone to do something like what she had done. He had loving people who'd raised him, but his 'siblings' had always treated him as different. Pushing that thought from his mind, he refocused on Mary.

"I almost died when you were born. They'd said I'd not be able to..." Mary paused, choking back the tears and pain.

Taylor rose and placed an arm around Mary's shoulders. That move saved him, for a bullet crashed through the window striking where he'd just vacated. Taylor pulled Mary off the chair and down to the floor. Then pulling his pistol, he raced toward the door. There, he cautiously opened it, poking his head out to look in the direction from where the shot had come. Seeing no one, he debated whether to chase the person who'd shot at him or return to Mary.

Mary saved him the trouble. She joined him at the door, shotgun in hand. "No one is going to shoot my son, not after I've just got him back."

CHAPTER 29

The shooting at Taylor made Edwin realize that things in town were heading to a showdown. It was time for him to make his decision. He would remain to help Taylor. As for Mary, well Mary was different. He wanted her to love him, go away with him, but she was determined to remain here. Could he stay to be with her? Perhaps it would be best to see what would happen over the next few days. The decision wasn't the best, but it allowed Edwin to focus on the present. It also gave him time to do what he could to mitigate the problems facing the town, and those he cared about.

"Edwin," Taylor called, "have you seen Thornton?"

"No, but I saw Jackson and his men ride in."

"Well, the three men, along with Curly, have been busted out of jail. I hate to think what is going to happen next."

Edwin understood. Despite the efforts the two had put in, and arresting Curly for the death of Wilson, the animosity between Thornton and Jackson had continued to fester. Jackson was still livid at Curly's betrayal, and blamed Thornton, forgetting that it had been Curly's choice.

"We best be on the lookout. I think this is the beginning of the end," Edwin prophesied.

"Believe you're right," Taylor agreed. "I'm heading over to check on Red, see if she's seen or heard anything of Thornton or his men."

Edwin grinned, he knew Taylor would ask Red about Thornton, but he knew that wasn't the only reason. Taylor had taken a liking to the girl and she with him. With things happening the way they were, who knew?

With Taylor heading over to the saloon and Red, Edwin decided to check on Mary. It hurt she still only saw him as her childhood friend, but such were the choices they made.

He was almost to the store when Thornton, Stu, and five others including the four who'd been in jail stopped in front of Edwin, blocking his path.

"Okay," Thornton addressed Edwin, "you have a choice to make, you can tell us where it's hidden or..."

Edwin knew he had no choice. "Since I told you I don't know anything about it, you may as well just kill me."

"Oh, you seem to think I care," Thornton sneered. "I could've killed you many times over, but that would get me no closer to what I want."

"Then what? That didn't seem to stop you with the others," Edwin started but was cut off as Stu started laughing.

Puzzled, Edwin started forward but stilled when he saw two men join the others with Mary held between them.

"That's what," Stu cackled as he moved toward Mary, all his hatred of her showing in his eyes.

Mary stood straight, almost daring the man to try something, despite her situation. Edwin was proud and terrified at the same time.

"If anything..." he began.

"Nothing will if you just tell us where you hid..."

"I've told you," Edwin gritted out, "I don't know what you're talking about."

"Stu," Thornton started but stopped short as Jackson and his crew approached. Stu had already started toward Mary but halted at a look from Thornton.

From where Edwin stood, things looked to get out of hand pretty quickly. And Mary was caught in the middle of the action.

Edwin, his mind racing, was trying to find a way to get Mary out of there. He saw only one way and putting thought to action, Edwin barreled forward. He rushed past Thornton, pushing Stu and grabbing Mary, forcing her back toward the store. "Get inside, quick!" Edwin urged, then pulling up behind the stumbling Stu, he grabbed the man's gun, using a technique he'd executed successfully in the war.

Once a weapon was in hand, he shoved Stu towards the others, clearing a path to the front and between the two groups.

"Okay gents," Edwin started, "before this goes any further," but his words died away as he heard the church bell and someone yelling 'fire' followed swiftly by the smell of smoke. The sound, followed by that smell of smoke sent frissons along Edwin's spine. His mind sped back to the gunpowder, bullets, and fire of battle. He needed to contain this situation, and himself before all hell broke loose. The folk of this town would need help with the fire if things continued.

Both Jackson and Thornton turned at the sound, then as they turned back, both drew and fired. The sound of the shots was like a signal, and from that point on, chaos reigned nonstop. Without a weapon, Stu ran toward the store, only to be stopped by a shot from one of Jackson's men.

"Stop," Edwin yelled, following it with a shot in the air, "you need to help with the fire," but his efforts were lost in the melee. A stray bullet just missed him as Edwin decided he'd best be able to maximize his effectiveness by helping with the fire. Turning to do just that, his movement was cut short by the sting of a bullet across his shoulder. He turned back around and saw Mary slipping out, heading in the direction of the fire. He prayed she'd be safe, realizing as much as he loved her, their friendship would always be the thing he could hold onto.

Hearing shots behind him, he turned and saw Taylor wading into the fray, his first shot taking Curly out of action. From where he stood,

Edwin's vantage point had a better command of the situation. Edwin decided to help Taylor contain this situation. He placed his shots carefully so that soon the guns were silent.

"Now, we can deal with whatever started this ruckus after we get the fire under control," Edwin told those still standing, "If you don't want to help, it's back in jail for you and pray the fire doesn't reach you."

Every man, except Thornton—who'd disappeared—turned to help. Unfortunately, the water supply was low, but a bucket brigade was started and the fire engine pump waded in. Each man did what he could, but a warm western wind had picked up, spreading the flames quicker than those fighting the fire could stop it.

Bear Claw showed up with some blasting powder. "Might be we could blast a fire line," he yelled.

"It might do more harm than good," Edwin yelled back. "Let's save it as a last resort."

Bear Claw nodded his understanding and moved to place the powder away from the flames.

Looking the situation over, Edwin yelled to the men nearest him, "Get some ropes to throw around these buildings and pull them down."

They got some long ropes from Mary's and threw it around the barbershop. It was a frame shack and, as they began to pull, the barber ran up behind them shouting, "You can't do that!" only to have his words cut short as Taylor pulled his pistol and yelled, "It's coming down, along with the next two on this and the opposite side of the road."

It seemed to work, but then another gust of wind blew through and the blaze jumped the fire break.

On and on people fought the fire for the next four hours. In the end, the upshot was they had to use the blasting powder, leveling a major portion of the west side of town. When it was all over, only Micah's, Mary's, the bank, and the church remained of the businesses. Most of the homes near the central part of town also burned to the ground. Some of the men, in striving to save the barrels of whiskey from the saloons, got carried away and started drinking the contents. Taylor soon put an end to that by having the mayor and his wife Agnes guard them.

They were all standing around when Thornton, having crept back in, took the opportunity to fire at the distracted Jackson, who fell with a shot to the leg. Thornton was turning his weapon on Taylor, but stopped, as Edwin and Taylor both fired. They both missed. Thornton ran off.

Jackson's men rushed to his aid while Taylor took off after Thornton.

"You make it okay?" Edwin queried Jackson.

"Yeah," Jackson grimaced, "kinda made a mess, but I was just so..." referring to the earlier confrontation with Thornton and his men.

"I know," Edwin said. "How about some of your men..."

Jackson nodded, "Sam, you help me out, the rest of you do whatever you can to help these folks."

Edwin and the rest of Jackson's men took off to help folks sort and save what they could, despite being exhausted. They had just moved a short distance when a spot started burning again. They all pitched in and soon had it out. Once that was done, Edwin suggested, "How about we head over and help folks best we can."

He heard some of them saying "Yeah, we tried to save the personal stuff, but it ain't much."

Others were bringing back the horses from the barn and livery, that they'd gotten out when the flames first appeared. Folks were hitching wagons and piling carts with what they'd salvaged, just in case the fire sparked up again.

CHAPTER 30

Mary stood outside her store as she handed people blankets, flour, and other necessities they needed to get through the next few days. She was planning what she might do next when Edwin walked up.

"Mary," Edwin began, "I've almost given you a special gift many times since I arrived. Now I think it's time for you to have it," he continued, "I know now, you..." he stopped. Looking down Edwin coughed, but whether it was from the smoke or something else, Mary couldn't tell. "Mary, I won't ask you to come with me,"

"Edwin," Mary began.

"Mary, let me finish," Edwin said, cutting her off. "You've got a life you've built, I understand that. Since we will probably not see each other again..." Edwin pulled up his head, lifting his hand when Mary started to interrupt again. "This town is dead, so you'll probably be going somewhere new."

Reaching into his left pocket, he drew out the locket he bought all those years ago. Slowly, his thumb caressing it one last time, he held it out to Mary, saying "I bought this for you when I was in St. Joseph, Missouri, near the beginning of the war. Carried it with me during all the campaigns. When I heard you married, well, it didn't feel right giving it to you. Now, well, I want you to have it. I love you Mary, but it's time for me to move on." Edwin paused for a breath, then continued, "I want you to have it. You have your life, but I am not a part of it, except as a friend. It may not be what I want, but you seem to have all you need. I want you to know if you ever need help or a strong shoulder...," Edwin left the rest unsaid. Instead, he pulled Mary into his arms, kissing her with all the love he'd carried through the years. Then he let her go "I will always love you, Mary. I carried the locket for many years. It was my way of holding onto a dream. Now, it's yours." With a sad smile, he turned.

Mary held the locket from Edwin, then looked up to say thank you, but he'd already turned and was walking away. Walking toward Taylor who was going to ride back to Kiowa Wells with him.

Mary watched the two, saying to herself, "It was a dream, you thought you..." as she opened the locket. Inside was a piece of lace. She looked up, trying to remember when Edwin would have gotten such a thing as a piece of lace. Her eyes returned to the locket in her hand and the lace inside. She remembered they'd been walking when she'd stepped on a patch of ice. Edwin had maneuvered himself, so she fell against him. He in turn had fallen, cutting his forehead. She'd used her kerchief to staunch the blood.

He'd kept that piece of lace from the kerchief all these years. For herself, what did she feel, was she in love with Edwin or just grateful for his friendship? Is that what she thought was love? Her eyes misted as she stared at the lace.

"Are you going to let those two go?" Bear Claw asked as he walked up.

She didn't reply. Part of her was pleased he'd gone. Now she could return to the life she'd so carefully built over the years. As she watched, another figure joined him. Mary knew it was Taylor, she could tell by the way he carried himself. As she returned to her store, she stood in what was left of the dream she'd had when she started her new life here.

In the space where her front window had been, was now an open tunnel for the wind to roar through, was what was left of that life. Looking around the town, she knew it was dying. The question she pondered, was she going to die with it?

Edwin had asked them both, her and Taylor if they wanted to return home with him. Taylor, still recovering from the stings and later the smoke had immediately agreed. "I could use a break before returning to work," he'd said. Now they were leaving, yet she still questioned her response to Edwin's offer.

Mary watched Edwin, his shoulders slumped from fatigue. He had done so much to try and save the town, to help her and the others. He was a good man. *It might have been different if we'd not been separated by the war*, Mary thought. But they had, and Mary didn't feel it did any good to live in the past. She'd decisions to make now.

Edwin was right, this town was dead. It could not be resuscitated. She watched as her neighbors and customers loaded what was left onto wagons and headed out.

Taylor, her son, went to help Edwin as he helped load young Bobby's mother's wagon. She'd lost her husband in the fire. Now she was going to Kiowa Wells, then to family back in Illinois. Edwin had told her she'd have a job in his store if she wished.

"Mary, what are you going to do?" Red asked, startling Mary out of her thoughts.

"I don't know," and she didn't. So many things had happened so quickly over the past week or so, she couldn't process it all.

"Taylor asked me if I'd like to go with him. I'd like to, but I wanted to say something to you before I answered," Red said.

"Why?" Mary asked although she felt she knew the reason.

"You know what I've been, and he's your son..."

"Red," Mary paused, then asked, "by the way, what's your real name?"

"Gertrude."

"Well, Gertrude, Taylor's a grown man, and if you two care for each other, then I've nothing to say in the matter."

"But, I admire you Mary, and I wouldn't do anything to hurt you."

"You would hurt me by not following your heart and making my son happy," Mary told Red, giving her a soft shove. "Now, go get him."

Bear Claw, hearing Mary's words, hugged Red. Red, in turn, hugged the big man back, then ran toward Taylor a huge smile on her face. Bear Claw turned and faced Mary, asking, "Mary-girl, are you going to let that man get away?"

"It's too late," Mary said, tears welling and shoulders slumping. "Besides, while he may have loved me when we were young, I'm old and not much of a catch today."

Bear Claw heard Mary out, then pulling the woman close, he hugged her. A chuckle rumbled in his chest.

"Mary-girl, that man loves you."

Mary pulled back, looking to see if Bear Claw was serious. "But how?"

"Listen, when you were so sick, you kept calling for Edwin. I knew it wasn't your husband's name. I thought it might be the name you wanted for your child if it were a boy. Now I know it's that man you're letting walk away. Besides, I saw the way he kissed you!"

Mary heard Bear Claw out, clouds clearing from her mind. "Yes, I love him, I always have, but as a friend. Now, well, I don't want to burden..."

"Now you listen here, not many get a second chance, the fact that he came running..." Bear Claw began.

"You really believe...?"

"Didn't he just say so? He opened up and told you the truth. Now, you got the courage to do the same?"

"I don't know," Mary answered. "For so many years...," she stopped. The image of Edwin tramping out of the snow and cold to find her beloved black and white cat, who had disappeared. She'd never really thought beyond his willingness to make her happy. Now thanks to Bear Claw's questions she realized she needed to answer her own preconceptions.

"Mary-girl, you somewhere else?" Bear Claw interrupted her train of thought. "That man's getting away."

"I don't want to hurt him. And my husband," Mary confessed, "he was a good man, despite what they say and what happened to him."

Bear Claw stood silent, he'd done what he could. He didn't want Mary to be hurt, but she was going to hurt herself if she couldn't figure this out. But would she figure it out? He knew how Edwin felt, how careful he was with not hurting those he cared about. The problem was it was about to bite him when it came to Mary. He couldn't stand by and watch, well the hell with her figuring it out. It was time he put thought to action. Bear Claw took Mary's hand, pulling her forward. "Edwin," he called, "wait up."

Hearing Bear Claw's words, Mary gasped and tried to turn back, but Bear Claw's grip and forward movement kept her progressing onward.

Edwin turned and saw Bear Claw pulling Mary toward them. What the old mountain man was up to he'd no idea. That it involved Mary was cause for hope and concern.

"All right, you two," Bear Claw began as he walked up.

"What do you think?" Mary began.

"No!" Bear Claw cut her off. "There is going to be no more hiding, second-guessing, or talking around the problem," he finished, crossing his arms over his chest.

Taylor and Red, standing off to the side, along with Rose and Lilly, shared a smile and a knowing look. Taylor added, "I'd like to see those two resolve it also."

So immersed were the people involved, they did not see the shadow creeping from behind Mary's store. A look of glee spread over the soot-covered face. *It is perfect, all those who have thwarted me in one place. It couldn't have worked out better*, the shadow thought. So pleased with the situation, an insane cackle escaped its lips. That was enough to turn the heads of Edwin, Taylor, and Bear Claw. Taylor and Edwin jumped in front of their respective ladies, pushing them down to the ground as the shotgun the shadow held expelled its load.

Edwin took the brunt of the shot, but movement and the fast, un-aimed shot saved him from a fatal wound, the buckshot grazing his back instead.

"You dirty—" Edwin began as he tried to move forward, but fell, as Mary cried out and crawled the short distance to where Edwin lay, crying his name over and over.

Bear Claw, seeing who'd fired the shot, took off with a roar, but his wounded leg and Edwin's outstretched arm conspired to trip him.

Although the shooter had started to run, seeing the melee before him, he turned back. He opened the shotgun, reloading it, as he advanced toward Edwin.

He kicked Edwin and turned him over. "Now, you will tell me where it is."

Edwin was pulled back to consciousness by the kick, hazily looked up. "Thornton, I don't know what you're talking about."

Mary rose and started trying to move Thornton away, but he pushed her back so hard she fell. Bear Claw roared and attempted to rise again.

"Don't tell me you didn't take my family carriage, accost my sisters and take off with the money and jewels hidden there," Thornton roared. "My mother told me all about what you did. Then when Chet said he'd found you..."

Edwin cast his mind back through the haze of pain. The only thing he could remember was in the early part of the campaign when they'd commandeered a wagon with two young women. They'd accompanied the women back home only to have their mother harangue them and curse President Lincoln. He'd felt sorry for them, but it was war and they needed the carriage. There was nothing special about it. "It was just a carriage, nothing special. We took the women home..." At that point Edwin was losing consciousness, remembering Thornton mentioning Chet.

"You lie, you lie," Thornton chanted as he prepared to pull the trigger, and in his haste forgot Taylor. Taylor, who had risen and with determined steps, moved forward.

"Thornton put down the shotgun," he ordered. "You are under arrest for attempted murder, among other things."

"Who do you think you are, you young—" Thornton snarled, as he continued squeezing the trigger.

Seeing no other option, Taylor aimed and fired.

Edwin lay on the ground. Mary was holding his head in her lap. She leaned over and whispered, "Don't die, I can't live without you."

CHAPTER 31

Two days later, Edwin, Taylor, Red, and the girls were preparing to leave. Edwin was feeling better. He felt the sooner he let Mary get back to her life, the better it would be for him, and her.

Mary had cared for Edwin, but nothing more was said of the locket or that Mary might come with him back to Kiowa Wells. In a way, Edwin was sorry, but also glad. He'd finally said what he'd wanted to all those years ago. Words that were the same today as back then, but he loved Mary too much to push her into anything. He was just glad she now had the locket, and he could move on.

As Mary watched Edwin and the others prepare to leave, Bear Claw's words started sinking in. The words she'd said when she thought he would die. Mary looked over again at Edwin. The joy and love she never realized he brought to her came rushing in. Edwin and her fishing in the inlets of the Mississippi. Edwin guiding her through climbing her first tree, always there when she needed him. How had she missed the signs? Now she was hesitating, embarrassed by her thoughts and her fear.

The store, her life, could she give that up? She had to admit she loved him, but... What was she thinking? The town was in shambles around her. Perhaps it would be like the phoenix and rise from the ashes, but the reality was, the town was dead.

Turning to Bear Claw, worry on her face, Mary asked, "What if he, I mean, I already said no?"

"Mary-girl, that man laid it all out for you. He even almost gave his life for you. He ain't likely to reject you."

Before Bear Claw had even finished, Mary was running down the street calling Edwin's name. Bear Claw was right, and even if Edwin were hesitant, she had hope that she could convince him of the rightness of their being together.

Edwin turned at the sound of his name. Panic tightened his chest as he saw Mary running toward him. Had something happened to Bear Claw? But as he looked, he saw the big man standing there, grinning from ear to ear. That look gave Edwin hope.

"Edwin, wait!" Mary called, "I need to talk—" Mary didn't get to finish her sentence. She'd reached Edwin and was folded into his arms. Some minutes later, the two looked up to see they had an audience. Taylor and Red shared a knowing look. Bear Claw, who'd moved up, was laughing, his eyes sparkling with happiness. The girls were giggling.

"You're all invited when we visit the sky pilot," Edwin grinned, his arm tight around Mary's waist. *Chet, whatever your reason for your actions, wherever you are, thank you*, Edwin thought.

Mary nodded, her face beaming, as she added, "It's taken a long time, but now the journey is over. And Edwin, there's a preacher still here in town."

"Why, so there is," Edwin grinned. Yes, it had been a long journey, Edwin thought. His chance had paid off and his prize was in his arms.

Wherever they lived, Kiowa Wells, near Mary's coalfield, anywhere, it would be special, if it was with Mary. Their life would be good. Edwin had learned—love answers when one takes a chance, no matter what your age.

CHAPTER THIRTY-TWO

AUTHOR'S NOTES

Although both the town of Kiowa Wells and Booming are fictional, they are based on stories and areas that are real. Both are located on the eastern plains of Colorado.

Kiowa Wells came into being and grew due to the building of the railroads, although towns like Kit Carson were around as early as 1838. Many of the eastern plains towns prospered due to the railroad. The area is one of rich history.

The story of the town of Boston, Colorado on the southeast plains was the template for the town of Booming. So many rich stories of outlaws, killings, and the burning of the town itself were a rich source of inspiration.

The character of Edwin's Civil War experiences were based on the letters soldiers has written to the newspapers in Iowa. Many of the smaller newspapers could not afford reporters so they depended on the local men who were serving to keep them apprised of what was happening.

AFTERWORD

Thank you for reading "Chasing a Chance". This is book two of the Kiowa Wells stories. Also on Amazon:

Book One – *"Josie's Dream"*
Book Two – *"Chasing A Chance"*
Book Three- *"The Outlaw's Letter"*
Additional work:
"Home for His Heart" - an Agate Gulch novella
"Never Had A Chance" – An Agate Gulch novella
"Gift of Forgiveness" – An Agate Gulch novella
"Lost Knight" - A Medieval Novella
Works in Anthologies:
"Under Western Stars" – Western Anthology
"The Untamed West" – Western Anthology
"One Hot Knight" – Medieval Anthology
"One Yuletide Knight" – Medieval Anthology

"One Christmas Knight" – Medieval Anthology

The author would like to thank the authors of Sweet Americana Sweethearts. It was their initial series Grandma's Wedding Quilt and Lockets and Lace that inspired this and the other Kiowa Wells stories.

ABOUT THE AUTHOR

Angela Raines is the pen name for Doris Mc-Craw. Doris is an author, historian, poet, and actor/musician. She moved from the historically rich region of West Central Illinois to the equally history-rich Colorado. The author of three novels and numerous short stories, inspired by the history the author researches.

Doris McCraw has published articles and blogs on the history of her adopted state of Colorado.

As an author, historian, performer, speaker, and poet, Doris moved from the historically rich region of West Central Illinois to the equally history-rich Colorado. Many of her works focus on the history that has surrounded her all her life. An avid reader Doris also loves to spend time in history archives, either online, in history centers, or in local libraries, looking for small, unknown pieces of history. Usually, these found gems find a way into her books, short stories, blogs, and non-fiction papers she writes. Her continuing project is document-ing the women doctors who lived, studied and worked in Colorado prior to 1900. Her latest non-fiction book is "Under the Stone: Early Women Doctors Buried in Evergreen Ceme-tery".

Doris writes in both Medieval and Western Romance, along with the Western genre. the thing that draws her is all of these time periods have extraordinary histories that just beg to be told. Sometimes Doris thinks the 'muse' may be asking too much, but then smiles and digs right in. The results? Stay tuned.